Christian
Island

Parables About Pride, Gossip & Discontentment

by Charles Simpson

Ascribe Publishing
P.O. Box 5726, L.I.C., NY 11105
http://homestead.juno.com/ascribepublishing

ISBN # 0-97000-48-0-X

In the Sea of Humanity, off the coast of Mammon, there's an island called Christian, where Mr. Saved Soul is the Mayor. Because of its beautiful beaches and abundant orchards, this island's reputation became much larger than its actual size.

Thus begins the first of three parables in which Mayor Saved Soul of Christian Island learns how to overcome pride, gossip and discontentment. The setting is on Christian Island, a tranquil place where the Mayor serves under the care and authority of the great King. Although the following stories are intentionally light and friendly, don't be fooled! The truths they contain are life-changing, and suitable for adults, teens and children.

CONTENTS

BOOK ONE:

Pride Attacks Christian Island

INTRODUCTION TO BOOK ONE

I've often studied verses from the Bible regarding the besetting sin of pride. In one particular passage God says to His people, "O Jerusalem, wash thine heart from wickedness, that thou mayest be saved. How long shall thy vain thoughts lodge within thee?" (Jeremiah 4:14) "Vain thoughts" refer to pride, vanity and arrogance. But it was the word "lodge" that really jumped out at me. Strong's Concordance shows us that this word in the original Greek refers to a traveler who comes to an inn, stays overnight, and then decides to remain there permanently. Aren't prideful thoughts just like that! As I was pondering these truths, this parable flashed through my mind in an instant. I can honestly say that the Lord gave me this story in less than twelve seconds, although it took twelve hours of non-stop writing to get it down on paper. (It also took about twelve months to finish editing it!)

The main lesson the first story endeavors to teach us is not how pride can enter in and cause one's downfall; but rather, how a person, through God's grace, can overcome this sin. The following poem summarizes the lesson in a nutshell.

Through the fall
of the wicked one,
We all have seen
the dangers of pride;

But even so,
whenever it comes,
We welcome this sin
unto our side...

Until the time
that we begin
To clearly and plainly see

The utter horror
of this sin...
Its wickedness
and its dishonesty.

ONE

In the Sea of Humanity, off the coast of Mammon, there's an island called Christian, where Mr. Saved Soul is the Mayor. Because of its beautiful beaches and abundant orchards, this island's reputation became much larger than its actual size.

One day, in the beginning of summer, the Mayor received a visit from a group of prestigious men from a faraway country. They came to see for themselves if Christian Island was as beautiful as they heard it was. Mayor Saved Soul usually had a staff member give tours to visitors, but since they had come from so far away, he decided to escort them himself.

As the Mayor led them up a cobblestone pathway toward the highest point on the island, he took a deep breath and said to himself, "This will be a perfect day for sight-seeing!" A refreshing fragrance lingered in the air from last night's rain. Ocean breezes continued to keep the temperature at a comfortable level in spite of the warm sunshine. "Yes," the Mayor affirmed loud enough for everyone to hear, "today is perfect!"

A light and friendly conversation developed as they casually made their way up the hill. "Everything is so carefree and peaceful here," one of the visitors thoughtfully commented. The others glanced around, nodding their heads in agreement. Signs of life surrounded them. Squirrels were running from tree to tree, birds were hopping through the grass, looking for food, and small groups of deer could be easily spotted as they roamed freely about. Everything truly was carefree and peaceful.

Near the top of the hill, the path took a sharp turn that led out to a scenic overlook built out of thousands of cobblestones. The visitors looked down on the scenery below, and were in such awe at all the beauty that it took their breath away. Standing there in silence for a few moments, they all overheard two turtledoves gently calling to one another from nearby trees. In the distance, songbirds of all kinds could be heard singing in the crisp, morning air. The hills were covered with flourishing apple and pear orchards and narrow, winding lanes connected numerous cottages throughout the land. They also noticed that the clean ocean surf could be heard and seen in the background. Everywhere one's eyes could go looked like a picture-perfect postcard.

"This island is known for its beauty and cleanliness," Mayor Saved Soul remarked, breaking the hallowed silence. Some of the awe-struck visitors slowly began lifting their binoculars, as others started focusing their cameras and taking pictures of the ocean, the beach, the cottages, the orchards, and even the cobblestone pathway they had just walked up.

"Look over there," the Mayor continued, pointing to the far distance. "That's the head of the island where the Beach of the Mind is located. Notice how clean it is!"

"Incredible!" replied one of the guests as he lifted up his binoculars to get a closer look. Someone else who had already begun to scan the shore with his binoculars noticed that armed guards apparently stood watch every three of four hundred feet along the entire length of the beach.

"They look so out of place on this quiet island," he thought to himself.

"Who are those men on the beach?" he asked abruptly. "What are they doing there?"

"I'm glad that you've asked," the Mayor quickly replied. "Those men are our guards who continually watch the beach like hawks. If any trash washes up on the pure sand, they immediately dispose of it. They also protect us from invaders."

"Invaders?" another visitor asked with amazement.

"Yes," Mayor Saved Soul slowly continued. "The one who previously owned this island would like it back. He used it as a garbage dump and, uh, I was his slave; and then one day King Jesus came...and..."

"Mayor Saved Soul," interrupted one of the visitors, who did not want to hear about King Jesus, "you're the greatest mayor I have ever met in my whole life! You're probably the greatest mayor in the entire world!" He put his arm around the Mayor and continued. "You've done such an amazing job of cleaning up a dumpy island and turning it into a paradise! You should receive recognition for what you've done!"

"Uh, to God...be the glory," the Mayor feebly replied. "Come with me," he said to the group. "Let me show you the heart of the island. It's the cleanest thing you've ever seen!"

As they all slowly walked down the hill together, the Mayor began contemplating how nice it would be to receive some recognition.

TWO

Mr. Comforter, the Mayor's personal counselor, lived in an apartment within the Mayor's residence. He was much more than just a counselor to the Mayor. He was his guide, his advocate, his personal assistant sent from the King to lead the Mayor into all truth.

Mr. Comforter was wondering why the Mayor hadn't come by so they could take their evening walk together. Their custom was to take two walks together every day: first thing in the morning, and before retiring in the evening. When he had received word that morning that the Mayor was busy giving some important visitors a tour, he thought the Mayor would be sure to make it for their evening stroll.

As he walked past the Mayor's study, heading towards his apartment, he noticed that light was coming from underneath the door. "Surely he isn't still working at this late hour," Mr. Comforter thought as he knocked on the door. Since there was no answer, he decided to go in and turn off the unnecessary lights. To his surprise, the Mayor was still in the office, standing near the large bay windows that lined the back of the study. The Mayor's arms were crossed and his back was to the door. He glanced over his shoulder at who had come in and went right back to his position facing the windows.

"Mayor Saved Soul, it looks like you've had a full day," Mr. Comforter remarked as he looked at the desk covered with papers.

The Mayor didn't even reply, obviously deeply engrossed in thought. Mr. Comforter walked over to where the Mayor was and joined him in looking out the window. He looked over in the direction of the heart of the island where the stairway of faith leading up to the King's throne room was still slightly visible in the night air, being illuminated by the glow of God's glorious throne.

"What did the visitors think of the stairway of faith and the throne room of King Jesus?" Mr. Comforter asked.

"We didn't go up there," the Mayor quickly responded. "We were...too busy looking at other things. We didn't have enough time."

"You didn't have enough time, to introduce them to King Jesus?" Mr. Comforter asked with astonishment.

"They wouldn't have been interested in seeing Him," the Mayor snapped back. "Besides," he added, "they didn't come to see Him. They came to see me. I mean, they came to see the island."

"But Mayor," Mr. Comforter exclaimed, "if it wasn't for the King, this island would still be a dump! We both know there's no other sight anywhere more glorious than the King's golden throne room."

The Mayor hadn't even heard his counselor's last remarks, he was so preoccupied with plans he was turning over and over in his mind. "For the next few days," the Mayor abruptly stated, "I'm going to be too busy to walk with you to the throne room. I'll let you know when I'm free to join you again." He then rudely turned around, sat down at his desk and began to scribble on the papers in front of him.

Mr. Comforter started to walk past the desk, to quietly and sadly leave the room. A crumpled piece of paper that had missed the waste basket was in his path. He bent down and picked it up to throw it away on his way out. The Mayor, thinking he was going to open up and read what was inside, jumped up in a panic and tried to grab the paper out of his hand. Mr. Comforter, shocked at his behavior, turned and faced him as he quietly dropped the paper into the waste basket nearby. For the first time their eyes met as they stood in front of each other. It was such an awkward moment. Mr. Comforter longed for the Mayor to open up and share about what had become more important to him than their trips to the throne room. He knew it would be disastrous for the Mayor to cut himself off from the strength and peace he received from his daily visits with the King. He also knew it would have to be the Mayor's choice to either confide in his friend or not. He just stood there waiting and hoping.

The Mayor turned away and sat down, and went back to working on his notes as Mr. Comforter proceeded to leave the room.

THREE

A few days later excitement gripped everyone on the island as news of a large banquet filled every conversation. The mailboxes throughout the land were filled with invitations. These invitations said:

YOU ARE HEREBY CORDIALLY INVITED TO A SPECIAL BANQUET THIS SATURDAY, IN HONOR OF MAYOR SAVED SOUL, WHO IS RECOGNIZED AS ONE OF THE GREATEST MAYORS IN THE WORLD.
COME AND PAY YOUR RESPECTS TO THIS AWESOME MAYOR. THE BANQUET WILL BE HELD IN THE HEART OF CHRISTIAN ISLAND AT NOON. THERE WILL BE PLENTY OF FOOD, AND EVERYONE IS REQUIRED TO ATTEND.

When Mr. Comforter received his invitation he was very grieved, to say the least, and went immediately to the Mayor to discuss his concerns. "Mayor Saved Soul," he began as he entered his study still holding the invitation in his hand, "you need to contact whoever's in charge of this banquet. If everyone comes, as the invitation states, that would include the guards. Who then would watch the Beach of Mind?"

The Mayor thought about this for a moment and then blurted out, "I'm not going to send out another letter saying a mistake was made on the invitation. Besides," he argued, "the guards could use a day off."

Mr. Comforter could hardly believe what he was hearing! "Do you mean," he slowly replied, "you are the one who is putting on this banquet, in honor of yourself?"

Too angry and embarrassed to say anything, the Mayor turned his back on Mr. Comforter, hoping he would just leave.

"I must, out of love and concern for you, give you this warning, Mayor," Mr. Comforter said. With intense seriousness he pulled out the Book of King Jesus from one of his pockets. He then slowly read:

"FOR MEN TO SEEK GLORY, THEIR OWN GLORY, CAUSES SUFFERING AND IS NOT GLORY." (Proverbs 25:27, Amplified Version)

The Mayor didn't respond and Mr. Comforter walked away with tears in his eyes.

FOUR

On Saturday morning everyone on the island was eagerly preparing for the banquet, everyone except for two people; Mr. Comforter, who was too grieved to go, and Mrs. Tender Mercy who somehow never received her invitation in the mail.

"Oh well," she thought. "I'm sure it was just an oversight. It's okay. I'd rather take a walk today, anyway," she decided as she noticed how beautiful the day was becoming. She quickly finished her morning dishes and then began watering the many plants she cared for in her small, sunny cottage as she thought about where to go. She filled a little basket with a few slices of bread and some fruit and said good-bye to her cat. She then went out to the lane that headed toward the beach.

The scenic road she walked on went through forests and over fields that were covered with millions of scented wildflowers. Mrs. Tender Mercy loved to stop in the middle of a cobblestone bridge that was built over a certain stream on the way to the beach and throw crumbs of bread to the ducks swimming below. "Nothing left but fruit," she replied to the quacking ducks she had just fed the bread to. As she made her way across the bridge, she noticed that the hill ahead was the steep one she loved to climb because of its magnificent view.

About twenty minutes later, and almost

completely worn out, she reached the top of the hill and stopped to catch her breath. As she sat down on a large rock, she noticed that the lovely beach was only a few hundred yards away. However, what really captured her attention and admiration was the stairway of faith that reached from the island right up into heaven! From where she sat, she could see it perfectly. Out from the heart of the island was a sparkling corridor, whose walls and ceiling were built out of glass and crystal. It was the corridor of conscience that connects the heart of the island to the stairway of faith. The stairway was so beautiful to behold! The stairs seemed to be suspended in mid-air. As the steps proceeded upward they got smaller and brighter. Mrs. Tender Mercy was admiring the view when suddenly a very bright light flashed upon the stairway! It looked like a bolt of lightning had come flashing out from the throne room and then remained on the steps. As the bright light began to make its way down the stairway, Mrs. Tender Mercy realized it was a shining, white angel who had just come from the presence of the King! As he reached the bottom step, she could see a royal scroll in his hand.

"I wonder who that dear angel is sent to minister to today," she thought to herself as he darted out of sight. A few minutes later, she picked up her basket and headed down to the beach, whistling a tune about the glory and majesty of King Jesus. Her heart was pounding with excitement at what she had just seen!

FIVE

The heart of the island was crowded with people of all ages who had come from every region. The roads were blocked off in the center of the town. Numerous tables were filled with all kinds of food, arranged in a huge semi-circle surrounding a platform about four feet high which was custom-built for the occasion. As the people gathered around the tables of food they could hear the speaker up on the platform making various announcements. They would load their plates as high as they could. Then they would make their way to the hundreds of chairs conveniently set up, facing the platform.

Everyone was so excited! No one could remember a day like this when everybody was together at one time and in one place. Friends and relatives shook hands, hugged each other, exchanged greetings and then settled down in their chairs to listen to the speaker.

As the noise of the crowd slowly died down, and as the last ones filled their plates and found a seat in the back, the voice of the speaker grew louder and clearer. Mayor Saved Soul was describing how he was able to keep the island so clean and beautiful. At different intervals, his staff, seated on the platform behind him, would break out in hearty applause at one of his statements, and soon everyone would join in with loud clapping and whistling. The emotions grew stronger and stronger. Then Mayor Saved Soul made some type of statement about the island being the best place in the entire universe. The crowd jumped to their feet giving the Mayor a standing ovation. The clapping, screaming and whistling went on for what seemed like a very long time. Some people who were ready to go get seconds from the food table, were wondering if the applause would ever end.

Suddenly, a flash of light as bright as lightning was spotted in the back of the crowd. It immediately caught everyone's attention as people turned to see what others were looking at. A beautiful, radiant angel, at least eight feet tall was steadily approaching the platform with a royal scroll in his hand, undoubtedly from King Jesus! A hush fell upon the audience as everyone felt so honored to behold such a sight. Some people thought the angel was going to present an award to the Mayor.

"Mayor Saved Soul, I have a message for you, from the King," the angel declared as he walked up to the front of the platform, extending the scroll for the Mayor to accept.

The Mayor was upset at being interrupted at a time when he had the attention of so many admirers. At that moment he also realized that he had forgotten to invite the King to his banquet! Feeling both anger and embarrassment, instead of reaching his hand out for the scroll, he snapped at the angel saying, "Tell the King I'll come by tomorrow to see Him."

Without any sign of emotion, the angel turned around and walked back through the crowd and past the tables and then out of sight. All eyes were upon the angel and as he disappeared, everyone turned back around and noticed that the Mayor was red in the face; red with anger and at the same time very embarrassed. He continued where he left off but the applause wasn't so loud and boisterous for several reasons. Some people were surprised at the Mayor's arrogant rudeness toward the angel, while others realized they had gotten a little too emotional before. However, the main reason why the applause died down so much was that people were more interested in getting seconds than in hearing the Mayor's speech.

SIX

Mrs. Tender Mercy soon arrived at the Beach of Mind. While walking on its pure sand, she abruptly stopped in her tracks. Mrs. Tender Mercy felt strongly that something was wrong, but didn't know what. She slowly and suspiciously turned to look all around her. At that instant, she spotted the same flash of light she had seen earlier making his way back up the stairway of faith and into the throne room. Even from so far away she noticed that the angel still had the royal scroll in his hand.

"How unusual!" she thought. "A divine message not received!"

SEVEN

The realization that the angel had an unsuccessful mission added to Mrs. Tender Mercy's uneasiness. She tried to overcome these awkward feelings by concentrating on the beauty of the waves rolling onto the lovely beach, but she couldn't shake it off. As she kept walking down the shoreline, she would often stop and stare out into the greenish-blue water seeing if perhaps a thunderstorm was on the horizon. Suddenly, from the corner of her eye, she spotted an enemy ship heading straight towards the island! She quickly ran off the beach and hid behind the nearest tree. As the ship got closer, she could read a name written on its side: WICKED THOUGHTS, it read. The ship came as close to the beach as possible. A number of small rafts were let down and many big, ugly, evil thoughts jumped in and began to row to the shore. Mrs. Tender Mercy noticed that the largest and ugliest evil thought, who appeared to be the leader, was a big, fat, evil thought of PRIDE.

"We're being attacked!" Mrs. Tender Mercy screamed. "Guards, guards, we're being attacked!"

But there was no response. All the guards were at the banquet! Mrs. Tender Mercy, who was much too tender to run, was much too merciful not to run; so run she did, straight to the heart of the island. When she got within the range of the crowds, she began yelling, "We're being attacked! Mayor, Mayor, we're being attacked!"

"What?" the Mayor called out from the platform. "Who? Where?"

"On the Beach...of Mind," Mrs. Tender Mercy cried as she gasped for breath. "A huge...enemy ship. Big, evil thoughts...coming ashore!"

"Guards!" the Mayor yelled in a panic, "to the beach!"

The guards all began running in the direction of the Beach of Mind. Then some of them who left their rifles at home, started running in the opposite direction. Many of them ran right into each other, knocking each other down. The crowd panicked and people knocked over food tables as they frantically tried to get out of the way of the confused guards. One of the women thoughtfully brought over a chair to where Mrs. Tender Mercy was. When she sat down, she fainted. She fell off the chair right onto the hard ground, being overcome with exhaustion. Many of the children then began screaming, thinking that Mrs. Tender Mercy had just died.

EIGHT

By the time the Mayor reached the Beach of Mind most of the guards had already begun shooting at the invading evil thoughts with their resistant rifles. As a bullet of resistance would hit the enemies, they would shrivel up and disappear and be destroyed.

"Resist them!" Mayor Saved Soul shouted. "Resist every evil thought! Let none get away!"

Soon, every evil thought had been resisted and destroyed, or so it seemed. In the midst of the fighting, unknown to the Mayor or any of the guards, three of the largest evil thoughts pulled out shovels and quickly dug a foxhole in the sand.

When the Mayor and his guards finally came out of hiding, thinking it was safe, one of the evil thoughts stuck his head out from the hole and shot at them.

"Look out!" the Mayor screamed, as he ran back under cover. "Apparently some of those evil thoughts have entrenched themselves in the sand," he continued, yelling loud enough for all the guards to hear. They were unable to hit and destroy those evil thoughts while they were in their foxhole. Because the evil thoughts knew this to be so, they refused to come out. Thus, there was a stalemate.

About an hour later the enemy ship pulled in its anchor and proceeded to sail away. The frustrated Mayor commanded the guards to diligently watch the foxhole while he decided to hurry back to the heart of the island to see if the banquet was still going on.

NINE

The next day the situation at the Beach of Mind hadn't changed. However, the three evil thoughts entrenched deep in the sand appeared to be harmless.

"There's nothing they can do," the Mayor said to his counselor who was standing nearby. "I'm sure they will eventually give up and surrender," he concluded.

"I totally disagree with you!" Mr. Comforter objected. "You need to go to the King right away," he advised, "and ask Him how to get those evil thoughts out before they cause more damage. No one has been able to patrol or clean the beach today because of them. Trash is already beginning to wash up onto the shore! Besides," he continued, "I heard that an angel came to the banquet yesterday to deliver a message to you from the King. You need to go see what that message was."

"Oh, He's probably angry at not being invited to my banquet," the Mayor blurted out, with an angry voice. "He's such an unjust God! Interrupting my banquet for no good reason!"

"But Mayor," Mr. Comforter objected, "King Jesus isn't like that! How could you even think that way about Him? You don't even know what the message was about!"

The Mayor rudely turned around and walked away. He went and found the commanding guard and told him to shoot the enemies if they ever came out and if they didn't come out, not to worry about it.

Meanwhile, deep in the foxhole, the three evil thoughts (a large, wicked thought of pride and two other evil thoughts) had dug down so deep into the sand of Mind that they hit solid rock. Then they took turns. One would watch for guards, while the other two would chisel out bricks to be used at the appropriate time.

TEN

One evening an unusually bad storm of affliction hit the island of Christian with the intensity of a hurricane. The storm clouds were so thick that they totally blocked the light of the moon and stars for the entire night and caused the island to become pitch black. In this complete darkness, the three evil thoughts surfaced out of their foxhole. Throughout the night they brought up onto the Beach of Mind all the bricks they had chiseled out and stored up. Unknown to the guards, who were on duty but couldn't see a thing, they constructed a strong brick castle on the edge of the island, right in the middle of the beach!

As the sun rose early the next morning, the guards were so surprised at what they saw! They all surrounded the castle and frantically shot at it with their resistant rifles, but to no avail. The enemy had gained a stronghold now, and mere resistance was no longer enough. When the guards tried to break down one of the walls by using their rifles as hammers, the three evil thoughts threw large bricks down on them from their position on the top of the castle. One of those bricks hit the commanding guard on the head and knocked him unconscious. The rest of the guards ran back into hiding while two of them carried their wounded commander back with them. A few minutes later, the evil thoughts defiantly raised the flag of the previous owner high above the castle!

The guards all huddled together in fear, not knowing what to do. It wasn't until late afternoon that the commanding guard regained consciousness. "Has anyone...told...the Mayor yet?" he slowly asked his men. Everyone looked around at each other, trying to figure out who should have taken charge, and why the Mayor wasn't informed. Immediately, one of the guards went and told Mayor Saved Soul about the castle.

"Why wasn't I told sooner?" he yelled at the nervous guard. "The sun is about to go down! Why did you wait so long to come and tell me?"

"Well," the guard stammered, searching for the right words. "Well, uh...the commanding guard, uh, was knocked unconscious for hours, sir, by one of their bricks, and no one assumed leadership, sir."

"AND WHY NOT?" the Mayor screamed.

"I guess because we were so frightened, sir. They really shook us up when we, uh, when we saw the flag of the enemy being raised above the castle."

The Mayor was about to yell again at the extremely nervous guard when Mr. Comforter stepped in. He encouraged him with some words of hope and instructions to the troops on the beach, and then dismissed him.

Mr. Comforter then turned to the Mayor saying "There's no need to vent your anger out on the guards. They're doing their best."

"So, the enemy thinks he's going to take over!"

the Mayor said with his hands clenched in anger and fear. "Well, he can't! I hope he can't. Oh no! What if he does?"

"Go to King Jesus, right away," Mr. Comforter advised. "He'll help you."

"No! Its okay. I'll be all right. It's just a castle. They can't harm us," the Mayor said, speaking more to himself then to his counselor. Mr. Comforter sensed that if he were to say anything more it would only cause an argument, so he sadly and quietly left the room.

ELEVEN

That same night Mayor Saved Soul tossed and turned in his bed as thoughts deep within his mind surfaced:

"There's nothing wrong with me honoring myself!" he thought. "I've done a lot for this island. How could King Jesus have allowed the enemy to build a castle out there on the beach without stopping it? What's wrong with Him? Does He REALLY care like he says He does?"

The evil thoughts in the Mayor's mind became deeply entrenched into his heart that night. Deep within himself he knew it was wrong to blame the perfect and loving King, but he had to blame someone.

"The beach is covered with smelly trash," he reasoned, "AND IT'S SOMEONE'S FAULT! AND IT'S NOT MY FAULT! SO IT MUST BE THE KING'S FAULT! PERHAPS I SHOULD BE KING OVER THIS ISLAND! I'D SURELY DO A MUCH BETTER JOB THAN HE'S DOING!"

As the Mayor tossed and turned, a cannon emerged from the top of the castle on the Beach of Mind, and throughout the long night, fiery cannonballs were shot into the heart of the island. These cannonballs did much damage to the heart of Christian Island. Hit the hardest was the corridor of conscience, which is the ONLY entrance from the heart of the island to the stairway of faith which leads up to the throne room of God.

Just as the sun began to rise in the eastern sky, there was a loud, disturbing knock on the front door of the Mayor's home. Since he was still in bed, he just lay there angrily thinking, "Who in the world would have the nerve to come around here so early?" As the furious Mayor listened, the knocking got louder and louder. Apparently, whoever was at the door knew he was home and they weren't going to stop until the Mayor came to the door. He reluctantly climbed out of bed and very slowly began dressing, hoping that the intruder would just go away before he finished so he could climb back under the warm covers. But the knocking wouldn't stop. So he headed to the front door muttering to himself, "I'm so upset at whoever has disturbed my sleep that I'm going to let them know just how angry I am!"

It didn't even dawn on Mayor Saved Soul that it had been years since he had allowed such hatred to fester in his mind. Apparent to everyone but himself, he wasn't the same mild-mannered, gentle Mayor he used to be. Slowly but surely, he had changed... drastically.

He grabbed the door knob and violently swung open the front door, ready to chew someone's head off.

"Mr. Comforter!" he exclaimed. "What are you doing here so early?"

"Come with me," he said in a commanding tone

as he turned around and, without hesitation, proceeded up the cobblestone pathway toward the scenic overview. The Mayor was about to tell him that he wasn't going anywhere before he had his morning coffee. Due to the apparent seriousness of the situation, he grabbed a sweater from the hall closet and soon caught up with Mr. Comforter. The Mayor noticed the pair of binoculars strapped around Mr. Comforter's neck, and somehow knew it wasn't for sight-seeing.

Even before they reached the top of the hill, the Mayor saw numerous columns of dark gray smoke ascending into the sky from the heart of the island.

"Oh my God!" he screamed as he began running towards the ledge. "What in the world has happened!" The Mayor put his hands against the sides of his face in astonishment as he noticed that a large part of the island had burned to the ground during the night. The dark gray columns of smoke rising from the smoldering ashes would reach a certain height in the sky and then spread out across the island. It created a huge, dreary cloud of unbelief over most of the land. The Mayor noticed that all the fruit trees were quickly withering as though they were suffocating and suffering an agonizing death.

Mr. Comforter came and stood beside the Mayor and very soberly said, "Look!" as he pointed to the Beach of Mind that was completely covered with filthy trash. He then pointed to the castle that had the barrel of a cannon sticking out from the top. The cannon was aimed at the burning ruins of the heart of the island. The frightened Mayor was dumb struck.

"Look over there," Mr. Comforter said, pointing to a huge barge racing towards the island. The barge was so large that, even from so far away, they could see everything that was on it: a billion tons of garbage, a million evil thoughts, a pile of large missiles, and eight exceedingly wicked demons; all worse than one demon who had lived on the island when it had formerly been a dump. There was a banner displayed on the side of the barge with some sort of message painted on it. The Mayor couldn't make out the writing, but as he turned to his counselor, Mr. Comforter was already handing him his binoculars. Through the lens of the binoculars, the Mayor quickly found the barge and focused in on the writing. It read:

I HAVE COME TO RECLAIM THIS LAND OF BACKSLIDER, WHICH WAS ONCE CALLED CHRISTIAN, WHICH WILL SOON BE CALLED REPROBATE.

YOURS TRULY, SATAN

"You MUST get to King Jesus," Mr. Comforter declared as he put his hand on the Mayor's trembling shoulder.

"No! I can't go to Him," the Mayor cried out as he turned his tear-filled face toward Mr. Comforter. "I can't go to Him."

"Mayor Saved Soul," Mr. Comforter gently replied, "did you see those large missiles of doubt on the enemy barge?" The dazed Mayor slowly shook his head yes. "If enough of those missiles hit it, it could destroy the stairway of faith which is the only link to King Jesus. With that link gone, Satan would surely take over and would assign those eight demons to rule this island for him." Mr. Comforter patiently paused, letting those words sink in. "Those missiles are too far away on the barge to hit the stairway. They would have to be unloaded and then shot from the cannon in the castle on the Beach of Mind in order to penetrate into the heart of the island where the stairway is. If we can get to the King before those missiles get to the castle..." He stopped, wondering if there was still enough time to get to the throne room as he turned and noticed how quickly the barge was moving.

"Please," the Mayor cried, as he frantically grabbed Mr. Comforter's arms and looked into his gentle face, "please, help me get to the King!"

THIRTEEN

Mayor Saved Soul and Mr. Comforter ran down the hill as quickly as they possibly could, heading toward the heart of the island. On the way they met a group of guards who were coming to report to the Mayor all the damage from the night before, and to warn them of the coming barge.

"Go back to the beach," the Mayor commanded as he ran past them. "Try your best to resist the enemy barge. We're going to the King for help," he said, yelling back to them without even slowing down.

The Mayor followed Mr. Comforter through the burning ashes in the heart of the island and into the corridor of conscience, where they were stopped in their tracks. The night before a cannonball hit the corridor so hard that it was almost completely destroyed. Debris and broken glass were everywhere. The entrance to the stairway was solidly blocked.

"Oh, no! I'm doomed!" the Mayor screamed.

"No, you're not," Mr. Comforter said.

"But this corridor is the only entrance to the stairway of faith," cried the Mayor. "How in the world can we get all this debris cleared out of the way in time?"

"There's only one way," Mr. Comforter calmly replied. "By finding out the cause of the damage to this corridor of conscience, and repenting." The Mayor looked at him with bewilderment, trying to figure out what he meant and how that could possibly help the situation. They began to look around and soon Mr. Comforter found a cannonball. "Here it is!" Mr. Comforter announced. "Look what's inscribed on its side- DELIBERATELY THINKING THE KING IS EVIL, WHEN YOU KNOW THE KING IS BLAMELESS." Mr. Comforter solemnly looked right into the Mayor's eyes and asked, "Did you think this thought?"

"Yes, I did," the Mayor confessed. "Last night, for most of the night."

"Mayor Saved Soul, the evil thoughts that you have allowed into your heart have caused your conscience to be defiled. You deliberately thought evil about King Jesus, whom you know is perfectly just and holy. Because of this, you don't have a clean conscience, and you cannot climb up the stairway of faith into the throne room without a clean conscience." He placed the cannonball into the Mayor's hand and turned aside, giving the Mayor time to think about what was just spoken to him.

The Mayor just stood there motionless for a few long minutes, staring down at the cannonball in his hands. Then he fell to his knees and began to weep, slowly and quietly at first, then with strong crying and deep tears. He cried in the direction of the stairway, hoping that somehow the King would hear him through the blockage. "I'm sorry for blaming You, King Jesus! Please forgive me! Please, have mercy on me," he pleaded.

Instantly, a loud noise could be heard from the other side of the blockage as the pile of broken glass began to move! An opening was being made as someone or something from the other side was pushing it out of the way. The startled Mayor jumped to his feet, expecting a huge angelic army to appear. To his surprise only Mrs. Tender Mercy walked through the opening she had just made for herself!

"Mayor Saved Soul," she calmly began, "the noise of that horrible cannon woke me up in the middle of the night. I came up to the throne room to spend some time with King Jesus. He heard your cries and sent me down to get you." She then pulled out from her purse the Book of King Jesus, and read out loud: "HE THAT COVERETH HIS SINS SHALL NOT PROSPER; BUT WHOSOEVER CONFESSETH AND FORSAKETH THEM SHALL HAVE MERCY." (Proverbs 28:13)

"The King is waiting for you," she announced with a smile. As the Mayor started to walk past her, she gently stopped him by touching his arm, and said slowly and very seriously, "Whosoever confesseth... AND forsaketh."

FOURTEEN

The Mayor then began up the stairway of faith like he had done countless times before, but this time he noticed that it was different. Instead of the stairs getting brighter and brighter as he went, they seemed to be getting darker. He stopped to catch his breath about halfway up, and it was then that he realized the darkness was coming from the dreary, gray cloud of smoke of unbelief that was smothering the island. As he looked up the stairs, instead of seeing the entrance into the golden throne room, all he could see was smoke.

"Perhaps there really isn't a God, after all," he murmured as the smoke began to fill his eyes, ears and lungs. "What am I thinking?" He said to himself as he began choking on the smoke. "I've got to keep going! The King is waiting for me," he said, remembering Mrs. Tender Mercy's encouraging words, as he held his nose and breath and ran through the cloud of unbelief.

FIFTEEN

As the Mayor kept going up the steps, the smoke cleared and he could see the entrance into the throne room ahead of him. The room glowed with the glorious light and splendor of the eternal God. In the very center, upon a majestic throne, high and lifted up, sat the King, the Lord Jesus Christ, shining with all the glory and radiance of the Heavenly Father. His eyes were as a flame of fire, His voice was as the sound of many waters, and His countenance was brighter than the sun at noonday. Hundreds and hundreds of angels stood around Him. They were forever singing songs of worship and adoration, as a beautiful, sparkling rainbow encircled them. Lightning and thunder were constantly flashing from the King as He sent out His Word in answer to various requests and petitions that ascended up to Him like sweet incense. Although the angels and the colorful rainbow were shining brightly, they could hardly be seen because of the radiant glow coming from King Jesus' face.

For the first time, the Mayor didn't even notice any of these things, as he was so consumed with his problems. He slowly approached the King as he had done so in times past, and knelt before Him with his head hanging down in shame and frustration.

"I'm sorry for blaming You, King Jesus," the Mayor began. "I'm sorry that I haven't come to you."

"My dear friend," the King lovingly replied,

"how I've missed you!"

Suddenly, the Mayor's ears were filled with a powerful, whistling sound that grew louder and louder. It was immediately followed by a huge explosion right behind him as an enemy missile of doubt hit the center of the stairway of faith. At the same time Mayor Saved Soul was hit with incredible doubts about the King, right there in the throne room! The battle was raging in the mind, heart, and soul of Christian Island.

"If the King really loved me," the Mayor thought to himself as he looked down at his hands that were trembling with fear, "He wouldn't have allowed the enemy to attack me like this! The King just stood by and did nothing, nothing but get angry because I didn't invite Him to my banquet." Much to the dismay of the King, the Mayor got up and began to back away from the throne. King Jesus tried to speak to the Mayor but he couldn't even hear Him.

"Maybe I should run out of here," the Mayor wondered as he retreated towards the stairway. As he was trying to figure out what to do, Mr. Comforter and Mrs. Tender Mercy entered the throne room from the stairway and noticed how distraught their friend was. Mr. Comforter tried to speak to the Mayor. He tore away from him and ran over to the steps leading down into the heart of the island, somehow thinking if he could just be alone for a little while then maybe everything would clear up. Just as he started down the first step, Mrs. Tender Mercy quickly approached him and placed a royal scroll in his way, dated the day of the banquet.

"I think you should read this," she politely suggested.

When he realized what it was, he suddenly came to himself, and seeing the condition of the island, his mind began to clear up. With part of the huge cloud of smoke clearing out of the way, he noticed that the barge had docked near the castle and the missiles were being unloaded onto the beach. He turned around and faced the throne room. Looking down at the scroll, he broke the seal, which had not yet been opened, unrolled it and read:

"DEAR MAYOR SAVED SOUL,
ALTHOUGH YOU HAVEN'T INVITED ME TO YOUR BANQUET, I WANT YOU TO KNOW I STILL CONSIDER YOU MY DEAR FRIEND. PLEASE DON'T LEAVE THE BEACH OF MIND UNGUARDED. IF SOME EVIL THOUGHTS WERE TO GET ENTRENCHED IN THE MIND, THEY COULD EVENTUALLY DESTROY THE CONSCIENCE AND FAITH OF CHRISTIAN.
IF YOU EVER BEGIN TO DOUBT MY LOVE FOR YOU, REMEMBER...I DIED FOR YOU, TO SAVE YOUR SOUL.
LOVE, KING JESUS CHRIST"

"I died for you." Those words rolled over and

over in the Mayor's mind. "I died for you! I DIED FOR YOU! I...DIED...FOR...YOU!" Every doubt, every fear, every evil thought toward the King melted away. The Mayor received deeper than ever before, the realization of the King's sacrificial love that was displayed at Cavalry where he bled and died for us all. The Mayor ran back to the feet of his King and wept.

"Oh, dear King Jesus, how wrong I've been! Forgive me for blaming you! You did try to warn me! You do care!" He looked up into the King's compassionate eyes and said with a panic-stricken voice, "King Jesus, the enemy is shooting missiles of doubt at the stairway of faith! Please, have mercy on me! Please, help me!"

Without any hesitation the King pulled out from His side some scarlet thread, saying to the Mayor, "You must destroy the castle, immediately. If you don't delay, you'll have enough time."

Mayor Saved Soul took the thread and quickly descended the stairway into the corridor of conscience and ran out into the heart of the island.

SIXTEEN

Mayor Saved Soul was relieved to notice that Mr. Comforter and Mrs. Tender Mercy were following close behind him. A few minutes later another fiery missile could be heard whistling over their heads. Then, such a loud explosion followed that it rocked the whole island, throwing the Mayor to the ground. He slowly got up with Mr. Comforter's help. Looking around, he picked up the thread he dropped when he fell. "How in the world can this little thread pull down a strong castle?" he mumbled to himself, as he looked around for a place to throw it away. Right as he was going to throw the scarlet thread into some nearby burning ashes, Mr. Comforter took out the Book of King Jesus and read to him:

"THE WEAPONS OF OUR WARFARE ARE NOT CARNAL, BUT MIGHTY THROUGH GOD TO THE PULLING DOWN OF STRONGHOLDS: CASTING DOWN IMAGINATIONS AND EVERY HIGH THING THAT EXALTETH ITSELF AGAINST THE KNOWLEDGE OF GOD, AND BRINGING INTO CAPTIVITY EVERY THOUGHT TO THE OBEDIENCE OF CHRIST." (2 Corinthians 10:4,5)

With that encouragement, the Mayor ran to the beach. All the guards had retreated into the nearby forest. The Mayor found the commanding guard and asked him how things were going.

"Not well, sir," he slowly began. "The demons have already unloaded so much garbage that the entire beach looks and smells like a filthy dump. The evil thoughts are entering the land from the barge so quickly that we can hardly fight them off. We're almost out of bullets anyway," he continued, getting more and more discouraged as he spoke. "Spending all our time and energy fighting off those invading evil thoughts, there's no one to stop the eight wicked demons from unloading their horrible missiles and carrying them to the cannon in the castle. I'm afraid another missile or two and the stairway of faith will collapse, and this island will be doomed."

"But guard," the Mayor replied, shaking him out of his despair, "I've been to the King! He's given me a weapon. I'm going out onto the beach, and I'm going to confront the enemy. As I lead, let's all charge the enemy together. Its our only hope."

The guard obediently shook his head and went to alert the rest of the guards. A few minutes later the Mayor ran out from behind the trees, holding high in the air the scarlet thread as he yelled, "IN THE NAME OF KING JESUS, I REBUKE YOU!"

The demons were in the process of unloading the third missile. One of the largest demons on the barge heard the Mayor coming toward them with the thread made from the blood of King Jesus in his hand.

"OOOOOOH! NOOOOOO!" he screamed. "LET'S GET OUT OF HERE! LOOK AT THAT

WEAPON IN HIS HAND! THE BLOOD OF JESUS! WE'RE POWERLESS AGAINST THAT!"

Immediately, the barge turned around and began to go full speed back to the Ocean of Hell from where it came. It turned so fast that all the missiles rolled off and fell into the water, never to be seen again. The barge then quickly disappeared over the horizon.

As the guards all charged the enemy, the few bullets they had left were enough to resist and destroy the remaining evil thoughts that were still trying to come ashore.

Now, the only thing left: the stronghold.

SEVENTEEN

Mayor Saved Soul cautiously walked up to the castle while the guards slowly surrounded it with their resistant rifles loaded and ready, waiting for orders. He then threw one end of the scarlet thread over the castle wall and held the other end in his hand. Amazingly, the thread somehow attached itself to the top of the wall. The Mayor then pulled with all his might, as he shouted:

"IN THE NAME OF KING JESUS, THE WEAPONS OF OUR WARFARE ARE MIGHTY THROUGH GOD, ENABLING ME TO PULL DOWN THIS STRONGHOLD!"

All the walls came tumbling down. The bricks, as well as the cannon immediately turned back to sand, crashing to the ground. All that was left were the three evil thoughts who had built and guarded the castle. They scrambled to their feet, and were about to run in every direction, when the Mayor quickly threw the thread at them saying:

"IN THE NAME OF KING JESUS, I BRING EVERY THOUGHT INTO CAPTIVITY!"

The thread wrapped around all three of them and bound them as if tied in heavy chains. The more they struggled to get free, the tighter the thread wrapped around them, until they finally stopped struggling. The guards, Mr. Comforter, and Mrs. Tender Mercy watched the Mayor approach the helpless enemies. He addressed the smallest one first.

"What's your name, you evil thought?" he demanded.

"My name is, 'God doesn't care about me.'"

The Mayor took the Book of King Jesus from Mr. Comforter's hand and read it loud:

"CASTING ALL YOUR CARE UPON HIM, FOR HE CARETH FOR YOU." (1 Peter 5:7)

Immediately, the evil thought shriveled up and was destroyed.

When Mayor Saved Soul turned to the next one he answered without even being spoken to.

"My name is, 'God is unjust,'" he said.

The Mayor turned to the pages of the Book in his hand and read:

"HE IS THE ROCK, HIS WORK IS PERFECT: FOR ALL HIS WAYS ARE JUDG-MENT: A GOD OF TRUTH AND WITHOUT INIQUITY, JUST AND RIGHT IS HE." (Deuteronomy 32:4)

The evil thought screamed, shriveled up, and was no more.

Finally, the last one. He was at least twice as big as the other two put together, and very ugly.

"You must be the leader," the Mayor interrogated as he walked around him, examining the bound enemy. The Mayor felt confident now, like a victorious general after a long, hard war. "You must be the cause of all the warfare we have gone through; the pain, the misery, the garbage on the beach and all the damage to the heart of this island. WHAT'S YOUR NAME?" the Mayor boldly asked.

The evil thought remained defiantly silent.

"I command you, in the Name of King Jesus, you evil, wicked, ugly, perverse thought, TELL ME YOUR NAME!"

The evil thought looked right into the Mayor's eyes and proclaimed, "My name is 'Mayor Saved Soul deserves some of God's glory, honor and praise'!"

The Mayor stepped back in shock. He was stunned and didn't know what to say. He looked around and tried to regain his composure. The beach was full of garbage. The heart of the island was in ruins. Mr. Comforter and Mrs. Tender Mercy stood there looking at him as if they weren't at all shocked by the name of that evil thought.

"MY NAME IS, 'MAYOR SAVED SOUL DESERVES SOME OF GOD'S GLORY, HONOR AND PRAISE,'" the evil thought screamed, breaking the silence. The Mayor looked over at Mr. Comforter, his eyes pleading for help.

Mr. Comforter said, "This will take a few scriptures," as he pointed out some passages to the Mayor. Slowly and forcefully the Mayor read out loud:

"A MAN CAN RECEIVE NOTHING, EXCEPT IT BE GIVEN HIM FROM HEAVEN." (John 3:27)

The evil thought fell over in excruciating pain,

holding its head as if he was just hit with an invisible baseball bat. The Mayor turned to the second passage and read:

"WHAT HAS THOU THAT THOU DID NOT RECEIVE? NOW IF THOU DID RECEIVE IT, WHY DOES THOU GLORY, AS IF THOU HAD NOT RECEIVED IT?" (1 Corinthians 4:7)

The evil thought squirmed on the ground in agony and pain; obviously greatly affected by the words, but still not destroyed. At his counselor's direction, the Mayor turned the pages once again. "This one ought to do it," Mr. Comforter stated with confidence.

Slowly, the Mayor read out loud: "WHO HAS KNOWN THE MIND OF THE LORD? OR WHO HAS BEEN HIS COUNSELOR? OR WHO HAS FIRST GIVEN TO HIM, AND IT SHALL BE RECOMPENSED UNTO HIM AGAIN? FOR OF HIM, AND THROUGH HIM, AND TO HIM, ARE ALL THINGS...TO HIM BE GLORY FOR EVER. AMEN." (Romans 11:34-36)

The evil thought screamed ferociously and then was destroyed.

EIGHTEEN

The Mayor turned around and looked at Mr. Comforter and Mrs. Tender Mercy with eyes of love and gratitude, as the guards behind them cheered and then began to disperse. Mayor Saved Soul started to walk off the garbage-filled beach without talking to his two friends. He didn't know what to say. Mrs. Tender Mercy gently touched his arm, just like she did earlier in the corridor of conscience, bringing back to his memory the words she had then spoken: "WHOSO CONFESSETH...AND...FORSAKETH HIS SINS SHALL HAVE MERCY."

The Mayor went to the road leading to the heart of the island, and then looked back at the beach behind him. It looked just like it did when he was a slave long ago. The entire island looked like it had once looked with the dark smoke of unbelief covering the sky. He vividly remembered when his life consisted of nothing more than carrying heavy piles of garbage off barges. A wicked demon with a cruel whip would beat him unmercifully every time he'd slow down. He turned towards the heart of the island, trying to shrug off those painful memories. He walked past the place where, long ago, he found a scroll of the Gospel of the King someone had thrown into the trash. He then remembered how excited he was when he first met Mr. Comforter who came to him in the garbage dump. He asked him if he wanted to meet the King he had been reading about in the scroll. He remembered how they walked along the same path, and how Mr. Comforter led him to a new master and a new life. He could recall how the smoke-filled cloud of unbelief had cleared, and how the heavy chains fell off as he first walked up the stairway of faith and stood in the presence of the King. The memories of all he was delivered from, not only in the past but also recently, filled him with the realization of his ingratitude and sinfulness. So deeply gripped with shame, he fell to his knees, covering his face with his hands.

When he opened his eyes a few minutes later, he noticed he had reached the heart of the island. The platform he had built for his banquet was only a few feet in front of him. It was the only thing that wasn't destroyed or damaged by the attacks of the enemy. As he stared at the platform, he painfully realized that he was the one responsible for inviting all the guards to the banquet; and by doing so, had allowed the destructive evil thoughts to enter the Beach of the Mind. For the first time it became clear to Mayor Saved Soul that the destruction inflicted upon the conscience and faith of Christian Island was a direct result of the sin of pride. The downfall of Christian Island, from beginning to an almost bitter end, was the complete responsibility of Mayor Saved Soul, and no one else. This fact profoundly broke the Mayor's heart to the core.

The scriptures he had quoted to the evil thought

of pride were now able to sink into his contrite heart as he allowed their truths to be engrafted into his soul:

"Truly, a man can receive nothing," he thought to himself, "unless it is given to him from God in heaven. Since that is true, it's wrong, it's dishonest, it's crazy to honor ourselves as though what we have received has really originated from us. Since ALL things have come FROM God, and have come THROUGH God, then without a doubt ALL the GLORY, HONOR AND PRAISE belongs TO GOD, and God alone, forever and ever! Now, I not only see the dangers of pride, but I can also clearly see the utter horror of this sin: its wickedness and its dishonesty."

As the Mayor wiped the tears from his eyes, he looked with disgust at the platform that he had ordered to be built for the banquet. "First thing tomorrow morning," he said to himself, "I'll have this platform destroyed, even if I have to come and do it myself."

The smoke then began clearing from the sky and a bright light beamed down upon the thoroughly repentant Mayor. At first he thought it was the sunshine. When he finally looked up, he realized the shaft of the light was coming out from the throne room: the King's way of once again inviting his friend into His holy presence. The Mayor slowly got up and brushed himself off as he walked into the corridor of conscience, up the stairway of faith, and into the golden throne room. He quietly walked up to the throne and got down on his face before the King and wept and wept and wept.

King Jesus was in the middle of writing a message on a scroll for another mayor of another island. When he heard Mayor Saved Soul, He handed His pen and scroll to one of the many angels who were attentively standing around Him. He then stepped down from His throne and got on His knees next to the Mayor and gently placed His right hand on the Mayor's shoulder, as a parent would do to a beloved child. That made the Mayor cry louder and deeper and longer. But between the sobs, he couldn't help noticing that the King of the Universe was crying with him! That gave the Mayor the courage to lift himself up and hold out his arms so his Lord and King could embrace him. They both cried together for a long time, holding each other as every wall between them crumbled away.

CONCLUSION

A few days later the inhabitants of Christian Island, as well as all of the Mayor's friends, relatives and associates received invitations in the mail. These invitations said:

THANKSGIVING BELONGS TO THE MOST HIGH, WHOSE WORKS ARE TRUTH, AND WHOSE WAYS ARE JUST; AND THOSE WHO WALK IN PRIDE HE IS ABLE TO ABASE. (Daniel 4:37) YOU ARE INVITED TO A BANQUET IN HONOR OF OUR GREAT KING, THE LORD JESUS CHRIST, MY SAVIOR, MY KEEPER, AND MY FRIEND; TO WHOM BELONGS ALL THE GLORY, HONOR AND PRAISE, FOREVER!

PLEASE MEET ME IN THE NEWLY RENOVATED CORRIDOR OF CONSCIENCE THIS SATURDAY AT NOON AND WE WILL ALL WALK UP THE STAIRWAY OF FAITH TOGETHER TO THE GLORIOUS THRONE ROOM OF OUR BELOVED KING.

EVERYONE IS INVITED- EXCEPT FOR THE GUARDS!

BOOK TWO:

Deliverance From The Sin Of Gossip

INTRODUCTION TO BOOK TWO

Gossip is one of those sins which is so easy to detect in others, so tempting to indulge in, and so hard to admit that we are guilty of. Some of us who would never think of falling into certain sinful acts, also never think twice about speaking evil of others, especially those we dislike or don't agree with. In this parable, Mayor Saved Soul of Christian Island doesn't realize the seriousness of his slanderous ways until God's chastisement upon him becomes severe. If only he would have been more attentive to the words from the Book of King Jesus!

God's Word is very clear concerning the sins of the tongue. We are instructed to "not let any unwholesome talk come out of your mouths, but only what is helpful for building others up according to their needs, that it may benefit those who listen." (Ephesians 4:29 NIV) Proverbs says, "A perverse man stirs up dissension, and a gossip separates close friends." (16:28 NIV) Jesus tells us that, "Out of the abundance of the heart the mouth speaketh." (Matthew 12:34) In the book of James we read: "The tongue...is an unruly evil, full of deadly poison. With it we bless our God and Father, and with it we curse men, who have been made in the similitude of God. Out of the same mouth proceed blessing and cursing. My brethren, these things ought not so to be. Does a spring send forth fresh water and bitter water from the same opening?" (3:6-11 NKJV) "The mouth of a righteous man is a well of life," Proverbs 10:11 says. Does a well of refreshing, life-giving speech flow out of our mouths to others, or does bitter water flow instead?

ONE

In the Sea of Humanity, off the coast of Mammon, there's an island called Christian, where Mr. Saved Soul is the Mayor. Because of the clear water that flows from a pure spring in the heart of the island, there's always plenty of cold, refreshing water for everyone to drink.

One day, in the early springtime, the Mayor welcomed some people from a faraway land. They spent most of the day sightseeing and in the evening came to the Mayor's residence for a casual visit. The group, seated on comfortable patio chairs on the Mayor's back porch, spoke to one another in quiet tones, not wanting to disturb the tranquil atmosphere. The crickets and katydids played their sweet music in the background similar to the way a violinist would calm patrons in a fancy restaurant. The Mayor entered the enclosed porch, carefully carrying four tall glasses in his hands. He placed them down on the table in the center of the room and proceeded to hand them to his guests. "This water," the Mayor began, "comes directly from the spring in the heart of the island. I'm sure you'll enjoy it."

He took note that there was one other guest to be served as he started back into the house.

"Mayor Saved Soul," he remarked, "I'm not thirsty. I'm fine."

One of the other guests, who had just taken a

quick drink of the water, enthusiastically declared, "That's the best water I've ever tasted! Even if you're not thirsty, you've just got to try it!"

"Okay," the man said reluctantly, as he politely smiled at the Mayor as he walked back into the house.

As soon as the Mayor left the room, the man spoke up. "Why in the world are you trying to flatter the Mayor so badly? Complimenting his drinking water? Give me a break! Are you gonna ask a big favor of him, or something? Trying to butter him up, huh?"

By this time the other three had finished their water, and they all agreed, that by far, it was the best water they ever drank. The Mayor came back in with two empty glasses in one hand and an extremely large water pitcher in the other. "Can we have some more?" the guests quickly asked.

"Sure," the friendly Mayor replied.

For the next ten minutes the Mayor stood in the center of the room, filling and refilling their glasses. He answered many questions, all of them about the water and the spring. "This spring wasn't always so clear," the Mayor admitted, grabbing everyone's attention. "One day the King put His hand upon it, and ever since then it has looked and tasted like this." He dramatically raised his glass high into the air as he spoke.

"King who?" someone asked, not because they wanted to know the King, but because they too wanted such beautiful water on their island.

"The King of kings, King Jesus!" the Mayor said proudly. "He's my Lord and Savior!"

"I don't need any Lord, or Savior," replied the guest who earlier accused his friend of trying to flatter the Mayor. "It's getting late and our boat is leaving very early in the morning. So I'm leaving," he angrily blurted out as he jumped to his feet. He spoke so rough, he even caused the crickets to hush. In the tense silence, everyone, including the angry man, wondered why he had gotten so upset. For a moment, no one said a word, or even moved. The other guests knew their friend well enough to realize that if the Mayor were to talk back to him, it would probably start a fight, right then and there. In the silence, the Mayor remembered the words his counselor had spoken to him earlier that day: "A soft answer turns away wrath, but a harsh word stirs up anger." (Proverbs 15:1 NKJV)

"I'm sorry for keeping you men up so late," the Mayor gently apologized. "Please forgive me. Tomorrow afternoon we're having an anniversary dinner at The Tavern on the Spring Restaurant. Why don't you all stay overnight, be my special guests, and leave on the ship that leaves tomorrow evening?"

Everyone in the group looked at each other, secretly trying to figure out how much more it would cost to stay at the fancy hotel for one more night.

"I insist," the Mayor cheerfully said. "As a

matter of fact, if you take up my offer, I'll pay your hotel bills for your entire trip."

"You've got a deal," the irritated one announced, apparently appointing himself as the spokesman for the group. He extended his hand out to the Mayor, and vigorously shook it; not as a gesture of friendship, but to make sure the Mayor wouldn't back out on such an unusually generous offer.

"I'll walk you to the hotel," the Mayor said, as the rest of the men rose to their feet. "That way, I can make sure the clerk sends the bill to my office."

"Thank you very much," some of the men said as they walked past the Mayor on their way out.

As they made their way down the brightly lit streets of Christian Island, the Mayor began to explain to the group that every home was directly linked to the spring. "Every water fountain, every sink, every house on this island has nothing but pure, refreshing spring water flowing through its pipes."

"Amazing," the entire group agreed.

"It's amazing because of the King," the Mayor acknowledged. He's the one who's amazing."

"Mayor Saved Soul," the quick tempered man interrupted, "I have a very important question to ask you." (Actually, he didn't want to hear any more about King Jesus.) "Since everyone gets their water from the same source, what happens when the spring becomes polluted?" he asked with a hateful smirk.

The Mayor thought to himself, "I can't believe

how hard it is to talk to some people about the King. Oh, well, tomorrow at the banquet, they'll have to listen to me. I hope the words I speak about King Jesus sink in; especially since it's gonna cost me a lot of money just to have them stay another night."

"WELL, WHAT WOULD YOU DO?" the man screamed into the Mayor's ear, furious that he seemed to be ignoring his "important" question.

"I don't know," the Mayor said in defense, not even remembering what the man asked him. Mayor Saved Soul then whispered under his breath, "Why don't you just shut up?" As soon as the words came out of his mouth, he wished he hadn't said them.

"WHAT DID YOU SAY?" the angry man yelled.

"I said, I have to be going," the Mayor replied. "I need to...go see someone before it gets too late. Take a left at this corner, and the hotel will be a few blocks down on the right hand side. Tell the clerk to bill me, and call me if there's a problem. I'll see you tomorrow afternoon at five o'clock sharp." He firmly turned around and walked back to his house, wondering if he had made a big mistake in inviting such rude people to the banquet.

TWO

Mr. Comforter, the Mayor's personal counselor, lived in an apartment within the Mayor's residence. He was always around to comfort, exhort and lead the Mayor into all truth.

"Why are you back so soon?" Mr. Comforter asked the downcast Mayor as he came dragging through the front door. "Weren't you going to walk your guests all the way to the hotel?"

"Yes," the Mayor said, "but one of them made me mad, and I talked back to him. We almost got into a fight, over nothing," the Mayor said angrily as he plopped himself onto the living room couch.

"No one can make you get mad," Mr. Comforter lovingly but strongly replied. "You *chose* to get angry. Didn't we spend time earlier today learning about how important it is to guard our tongues? Did you forget that a soft answer can turn away wrath?"

"Quit treating me like a child," the Mayor blurted out with the intensity of a toddler on the verge of a serious temper tantrum. "I'm so tired of trying to always say just the right words to everybody," he yelled. "People don't always say nice things to me, you know!"

"But the blessings of godly speech far outweigh the consequences of having a loose tongue, my dear Mayor. The Book of King Jesus promises us that because of the pureness of the lips, the King shall be your friend." (Proverbs 22:11)

The Mayor wasn't even listening. He was still boiling over with frustration at how his guest had treated him. "I bet that man doesn't even have a job. He's such a low-life. I'm gonna call the hotel clerk and tell him to not allow him to make any long distance calls. Otherwise, he'll probably call all over the world, at my expense!"

The Mayor started to storm out the room, but not before Mr. Comforter stopped him. "Don't talk that way about someone you just met today, Mayor. Just because he may have a temper problem doesn't mean he's a criminal. You're getting close to slandering him."

The Mayor put his head down, in apparent remorse over what he was doing. He was faking it, however. In his heart, he was just hoping his counselor would stop lecturing him.

Mr. Comforter continued, "The Book of the King clearly warns us to be quick to hear, slow to speak, and slow to wrath. I've written this down on a scroll, along with all the other truths that we've been studying lately about taming the unruly tongue. I suggest you read these, meditate upon them and let them sink deep inside. Okay?"

The Mayor seemed to gratefully accept the scroll from Mr. Comforter's outstretched hand.

"God knows, the repercussions of evil speaking can be disastrous," Mr. Comforter admonished. "I hope you won't have to learn the hard way, my friend."

The Mayor left the room and went to his study. He haphazardly threw the scroll into one of his messy desk drawers with no intention of looking at it any time soon. He picked up his phone, and spent the next half hour telling the hotel clerk what a creep the quick-tempered man was.

THREE

The following day the temperature on the island was unusually hot for early spring. However, by the time the anniversary dinner began, the cool breeze from the ocean was refreshing everyone. Since it was sure to be a comfortable evening there was a large turnout at The Tavern on the Spring. The large building was constructed right next to the mouth of the spring in the heart of Christian Island. What made it everyone's favorite place to eat was the huge patio that was cleverly built around much of the restaurant. Since it was on a hill, the patio had many layers to it, each section going farther and farther down. The tables were spread out in such a way that whoever was seated at the top layer could easily address the entire restaurant crowd. Mayor Saved Soul and Mr. Comforter were seated at the top, and next to them a table was reserved for Mrs. Tender Mercy and Mr. and Mrs. Joy and their family.

In the next section the waiters were instructed to reserve tables for the visitors whom the Mayor had personally invited. It was a good thing those tables were reserved, because by five fifteen every available seat was taken. The many waiters and waitresses were already busy serving the soup and salads like busy bees. The melodious sound of the spring could be heard as it bubbled out pure water from the source, pouring it down the hill. A large banner draped along the entire length of the restaurant's outside wall boldly stated, "THANKS TO KING JESUS FOR FIVE WONDER - FILLED YEARS!"

Mrs. Tender Mercy was trying to calm her niece down, who looked as if she was on the verge of crying. "But, Aunt Mercy," she whimpered, "you promised, and my boat leaves early tomorrow morning; and I don't know when I'll ever be able to visit you again."

"I know, honey," she said sympathetically. "But I also promised the Mayor a long time ago that I'd be here. This is a very special occasion for him."

"All right," her niece finally conceded. "Maybe next time," she said as she tried to form a smile on her sad face.

The Mayor got up from his seat and squatted down between Mrs. Tender Mercy and her niece. "Everything okay?" he asked.

"Yes, sir," the niece politely replied. "This is a lovely restaurant, sir."

"Yes, it really is," he remarked as he looked around and then stood to go back to his seat. Mrs. Tender Mercy touched his arm, and said. "Mayor, I have a big favor to ask of you."

"Yes?" he asked with genuine concern.

"I promised my niece last year that the next time she visited me I would take her to the beach. She lives on the mainland, you know. She has to leave early tomorrow morning. I didn't realize her visit would fall on the day of the anniversary." She paused for a moment, aware that her question was taking a long time to get out. "Would you mind if we leave a little early?"

"That's fine," the Mayor chuckled as he patted the niece's head. "As a matter of fact," he paused and turned to a passing waiter. "Waiter," he called out, "put my two friend's dinners in take out containers, along with utensils, napkins, and a tablecloth."

"A tablecloth, sir?" the waiter asked with surprised amusement.

"Yes, and hurry," the Mayor said. "They need to be going in a few minutes."

"Thank you so much," Mrs. Tender Mercy said.

"Thank you, sir," her niece echoed.

A few short minutes later, the waiter handed a large bag to the Mayor, who in turn gave it to Mrs. Tender Mercy, saying, "Have a great picnic on the beach. You should still have a few hours of sunlight left."

FOUR

After they finished their scrumptious meal, Mrs. Tender Mercy and her niece carefully shook off all the sand on the tablecloth, neatly folded it and placed it back into the bag. "Let's go for a walk," Mrs. Tender Mercy suggested.

"Aunt Mercy, can I take my shoes off and wade in the water a little?"

"Only if you're really careful not to get your dress wet."

"I promise," her niece declared as she threw off her shoes and ran into the shallow water.

As Mrs. Tender Mercy looked around, she noticed the beach was empty, except for a few guards scattered here and there. These men had the job of cleaning up any trash that would try to wash up onto the shore of the Beach of Mind. They also had the responsibility of watching out for enemy ships carrying demonic thoughts that might try to invade the island.

"I guess just about everyone is at the restaurant," Mrs. Tender Mercy uttered to herself.

Suddenly, from somewhere way out in the ocean, a huge explosion occurred. It came from deep within the Ocean of Hell, which is a few hundred miles south of the land of Mammon. It caused the guards to instinctively point their resistant rifles out in the direction of the water. Mrs. Tender Mercy's niece screamed and ran into her Aunt's protective arms. She dug her head into her Aunt's bosom, afraid to look at whatever made such an incredible noise.

The explosion caused a tremendously large tidal wave to develop way offshore. Just as Mrs. Tender Mercy was about to start running toward the hills, she noticed that the closer the wave got the smaller it became. By the time it reached the island it was just an unusually large wave. The frightened girl, still clinging tightly to her Aunt, looked up as the wave came rolling in.

"Look! There's a bottle with a cork in it," she proclaimed.

"Where?" Mrs. Tender Mercy asked.

"Right over there," she pointed. "On the top of that big wave. Aunt Mercy, maybe it has a message inside!"

The wave slapped against the sharp rocks, and then a calm quickly settled back down upon the lovely beach.

The niece hastily put her shoes back on, asking with extreme excitement, "Can I go and see if there's a message in the bottle? Please, can I? Please? Please?"

"Let me go with you," Mrs. Tender Mercy said, as she grabbed her hand and ran in the direction of where the bottle seemed to have washed ashore.

It only took a few minutes to find the dark brown bottle amidst the light colored rocks and sand. "Here it is," the niece said with noticeable disappointment. "It must have broken when it hit the rocks. I guess nothing was inside."

"What is that?" Mrs. Tender Mercy said, pointing down to what looked like lines sketched in the sand. A second later, another wave of water came through and it was gone.

"What was that?" the curious niece asked.

"Well, I'm not certain. It sure looked like the tracks of a snake! It appears as though it crawled out from the bottle and then went into that hole over there."

"Could a snake have actually been in that bottle?" her niece asked.

"What a strange message!" Mrs. Tender Mercy thought out loud, being so puzzled that she didn't even hear her niece's question. She felt as she just witnessed an event that something or someone did not want anyone to see; something dark and evil.

FIVE

As the last ones at the restaurant were being served their desserts, Mayor Saved Soul's voice could be heard on the elaborate intercom system.

"I want to thank everyone for coming to this special dinner," he began. "Today we are celebrating a very wonderful occasion. But before I get to that, let me share some background information."

The quick-tempered man, seated in the front on the second level with the rest of the guests, turned to his group and declared, "This is gonna be long, and boring."

"Shhhhh," one of the nearby waiters insisted.

"We all know," the Mayor continued, "that this island is one of the most beautiful places on earth. We are blessed with immaculate beaches, fruitful orchards and also this clear spring. The water that flows out from here is known throughout the world as being the best tasting, anywhere. We are able today to enjoy all these rich blessings only because of the generous mercy of our great King!"

He then stopped, giving everyone a chance to show their appreciation to the King with a hearty round of applause, and with a little bit of whistling thrown in here and there. The front row guests were clearly the only ones on the entire patio who weren't clapping. Once they realized everyone was noticing them, they enthusiastically joined in.

The Mayor took a deep breath and continued. "Many years ago, believe it or not, this lovely island was nothing more than a huge, filthy garbage dump. It was completely owned by satan and I was one of his helpless slaves. My deplorable life consisted of nothing more than carrying tons and ton of smelly garbage off barges that came from the land of Mammon. I still have the scars on my back from when wicked demons would whip me viciously whenever I'd even slow down for a moment." He stopped and pulled out his handkerchief to wipe the tears of gratitude that were flowing down his cheeks. Everyone was deeply moved, especially the guests on the second patio. They had never heard such a testimony before.

The Mayor turned toward his left and pointed, speaking with intense emotion. "Right over there, about five years ago, I found a scroll of the Gospel of the King that someone had apparently thrown away into the garbage. Every evening when the demons would leave me for the night, I would pull it out from under my blanket and read about King Jesus. I learned about His incredible birth and life, and His sacrificial death. One evening, as I was reading, a miraculous thing occurred. A golden stairway of faith began to rise into the heavens from the heart of the dump. Satan was furious when he saw the stairs beginning to form. He personally came and tried to beat me to death with his own hands. For hours he pounded me so hard I thought I would lose my mind. Suddenly, as the sun began to rise, he disappeared."

"The next thing I remember was this Person on my left coming to me," referring to Mr. Comforter. "When he asked me if I wanted to meet the King I had been reading about I said to him, 'I think so.' It was all so new to me. He then helped me up and led me over to the stairway of faith. I was a little afraid to walk up the steps; afraid they might not support the weight of all the chains around my ankles, my arms and my neck. But as we started up, the chains fell off, one by one. When we reached the golden throne room, I walked over to King Jesus and asked Him to forgive me of all my sins."

Just then, an extremely bright light emerged from the bottom of the hill. An angel was walking up the steps that connected the layers of the patio, steadily approaching the surprised Mayor! When he got to the top, he handed the Mayor a royal scroll, saying, "A message for you, from the King."

"Thank you," he replied.

"Wow! A real, live angel," the quick-tempered man yelled out.

As the angel jumped into the air and began to fly away, the Mayor opened up the scroll and eagerly read the message. Everyone sat there in silence, not moving an inch. Even the waiters and waitresses stood still, frozen with amazement.

Mr. Comforter came over behind the Mayor and looked at the message. He then forcefully whispered into his ear, "Mayor, do not read this message out loud. Continue your testimony for a few more minutes and then conclude with an invitation to pray for whoever here needs to meet the King."

"Wow! A message from a king, hand-delivered by an angel," the quick-tempered man screamed out again, breaking the silence.

Mayor Saved Soul felt torn. He wanted to show his guests that he knew the King personally. He especially wanted to impress the quick tempered man.

"I'll show him," he thought to himself. "He'll think twice before he yells at me again. He'll have to respect a person who gets hand-delivered messages from heaven!"

The Mayor cleared his throat in the microphone and announced, "I'm going to conclude by leading everyone in a prayer to receive the same forgiveness from the King that I have received." He then turned and smiled at Mr. Comforter. "But first, I'm going to read this message to all of you that I just received, directly from the King!" Awe swept over the captive audience.

He dramatically lifted up the scroll and forcefully read into the microphone, "Dear Mayor Saved Soul, Congratulations on your five-year anniversary! Please remember the Mayor of your neighboring island in your prayers. Mayor Dee Livered is having serious family problems. Please have as many people pray for him as you possibly can. Thanks and take care. Sincerely, The King."

The message fell flat as it hit the anxious audience. All it produced was an intense curiosity as to what kind of family problems Mayor Dee Livered was having. Rumbling noises could be heard throughout the restaurant as people turned around to those nearby, asking each other if they knew what was happening with Mayor Dee Livered. "Has his wife left him? Are they getting a divorce? How long have they had problems?"

The Mayor, trying to regain the attention of the distracted crowd, forcefully spoke into the microphone. "Now, Mr. Comforter is going to come and lead us in a prayer." When the Mayor turned to Mr. Comforter, he was shocked to find out that he was gone. As the scroll was being read, Mr. Comforter became so grieved that he just had to get up and walk away.

The excited visitors then jumped to their feet and came running to the Mayor. He dropped the scroll next to his chair and came over to the crowd. One or two of the visitors actually came forward for prayer, but they were drowned out by all the loud questions.

"Are Mayor Dee Livered and his wife getting counseling? Have they gotten a divorce yet?" In all the excitement the quick tempered man actually grabbed the Mayor's shirt sleeve and almost pulled him off the patio, yelling into his face, "HAVE THEY GOTTEN A DIVORCE YET?"

The angry Mayor yelled back even louder, "NO, THEY HAVEN'T GOTTEN THE DIVORCE YET!"

The whole crowd heard him. According to the Mayor's official remarks Mayor Dee Livered was definitely getting divorced from his wife. It was only a question of when.

"This has turned into nothing more than a frantic press conference," the frustrated Mayor said to himself, as he walked back to his seat to get away from the curious crowd. He walked over to the scroll on the ground, and instead of picking it up as he should have, he kicked it with all his might, and with all the frustration that was in him. It went flying off the platform and up into the rocks, near the mouth of the spring. "I shouldn't have done that," the Mayor instantly realized. "I'd better go and find it."

As the crowd mingled with each other and began to leave the restaurant, the Mayor went behind the platform and carefully climbed the rocks in the direction the scroll had landed. As he reached the top of the rocks, he discovered a small hole a few inches wide, perhaps large enough for the scroll to fall into. He could hear water bubbling up from within the rocks. It was deep and dark and directly above the very mouth of the spring in the heart of the island.

"I sure hope that scroll didn't fall in there," he said to himself as he nervously kept searching. About a half hour later he concluded that it must have fallen down into that hole in the rocks. "Oh well. I'm sure it won't hurt anything," he hopefully thought as he started for home. He would have thought differently had he seen what happened when the scroll hit the water. The paper turned into snake skin and went from a bright white to a deep, grayish-black. A few hours later, tiny grayish-black specks began slowly, unnoticeably, seeping out from the spring into the pipes that lead to every water fountain, sink and home on the island.

SIX

The next morning, as people throughout the entire island opened the faucets in their bathrooms and kitchens, the contaminated water began to flow into all the homes. At the same time, people all over the region were on the phone with one another, praying for Mayor Dee Livered. At least that's how the conversations would begin. "We need to pray for Mayor Dee Livered and his family," they would say. "I was told by reliable sources that he and his wife are on the verge of a divorce." From that point the conversations turned into gossip, slander and rumors galore. There were reports that Mayor Dee Livered was guilty of all sorts of crimes, from tax evasion to bank robbery. It was reported that his wife had moved back to her mother's and they were in a terrible custody battle for the kids. No one realized the fact that as the vicious and totally false rumors spread, so did the contaminated water.

Soon, many of the children on the island became extremely ill from the drinking water. The doctors gave them various kinds of medicine, but nothing helped. "I'm not sure what's happening," they all would eventually say. "You're going to have to get your child off this island until we discover the source of the problem," the doctors would tell the parents. Thus, a mass exodus began.

One day, Mr. Joy came to see the Mayor. He

was one of his best and most trusted friends. The Mayor was heartbroken when his close friend announced that he and his family were moving away. "We just can't take it any longer. Our children are constantly sick," he said.

"Where are you moving to?" the Mayor asked.

"We thought we'd just go over...perhaps to Mayor Dee Livered's island. It's the nearest island to us, and maybe when someone discovers what the problem is, we could easily return."

"You can't be serious about moving to that wicked man's island," the Mayor protested. Thus, the gossip would spread like wildfire; that is, like contaminated water. The Mayor talked everyone into moving far away to the mainland of Mammon, instead of the convenient, nearby island where Mayor Dee Livered lived.

The day arrived when the Mayor accompanied the Joy family down to a ship that was waiting for them at the beach. The whole family was leaving: Mr. and Mrs. Joy with all their little children- Laughter, Giggles, Happiness, and Merry. As the Mayor watched the ship slowly sail away, he immediately noticed the difference on Christian Island. Joy was gone. Happiness and Laughter were gone. Soon afterwards, Mr. Peace left as well as the entire Hope family. The downcast Mayor knew something drastic had to be done.

"We must ask the King what the root problem

is," Mr. Comforter advised.

"Yes," the Mayor agreed. "Let's go to His throne of grace and ask for His mercy and grace to help us in this time of desperate need."

Together they walked into the heart of the island and into the corridor of conscience. From there they entered the stairway of faith that reached right into heaven. As they entered into the golden throne room at the top of the steps, they could hear soft, melodious music coming from hundreds of angels playing harps in perfect unison. The room was filled with the glorious light and splendor of the eternal God. In the very center, upon a majestic throne, high and lifted up, sat the King, the Lord Jesus Christ, shining with all the glory and radiance of the Heavenly Father. His eyes were as a flame of fire, His voice was as the sound of many waters, and His countenance was brighter than the sun when it shines in its full strength.

The Mayor had never stopped his routine of making daily visits to the King. It was one of Mr. Comforter's main duties-to escort the Mayor to the throne room once, or even sometimes twice a day. But lately it had become just a routine. The Mayor got less and less out of the visits. He could no longer look into the loving, piercing, eyes of his King. His utter holiness convicted the Mayor of his sinfulness. Deep in his heart he knew he had allowed many lies and evil things to proceed out of his mouth. Sadly, he was convicted enough to feel uncomfortable in the Lord's presence, but not convicted deeply enough to cry out to the Lord for cleansing.

At least he had enough sense to cry out to the Lord for help as the situation became desperate. "Please, please show me why so many people on this island are getting sick. Please help me dear King Jesus."

"Of course I'll help you, my precious child. Come over here and let me give you a hug," the compassionate King said.

The Mayor reluctantly came into his arms like a child would do to an overbearing relative, whose hugs and kisses are tolerated but not welcomed. The King gave him a big squeeze that began to melt the Mayor's overburdened heart. He wanted to squeeze the King in reply and just cry in his arms for a while, but he held back, for some reason.

The King put His strong, but gentle hands on the Mayor's shoulders and pulled him away just enough to look deep into his eyes. The piercing eyes of the Lord were absolutely overflowing with love. They also revealed the fire of holiness so much that the Mayor felt as if his soul was being examined with a microscope. He felt completely transparent under the Lord's gaze. "The reason why people are getting sick," the King began, "is because the drinking water is contaminated. In order for the water to be cleansed, you must take a good look at what is coming out of the mouth of the spring. That's where the problem is, my dear Mayor."

"Thank you! Thank you so much," the Mayor said as he abruptly walked over to the stairs leading back to the island. The King had more to say, but the Mayor couldn't handle those penetrating eyes any longer. As he descended the steps, the King added, "Don't worry, Mayor Saved Soul. I'll see you through this hard time."

SEVEN

The Mayor ran right to the spring and knelt down to get a scoop of water in his hands. "Why didn't somebody have the common sense to check the water supply? Anyone could see that this water is contaminated! Look at all these dark, little specks," the Mayor angrily barked at Mr. Comforter, who had accompanied him. "Do I have to figure out everything on this island? I must have a bunch of stupid idiots living here with me," he continued.

"Mayor Saved Soul, look!" Mr. Comforter exclaimed, pointing to the mouth of the spring. "The more you allow ungodly words to come out of your mouth, the darker the water gets that's flowing out from the mouth of the spring!"

"That's crazy," the Mayor yelled. "One thing has nothing to do with the other."

"Oh, yes it does," Mr. Comforter calmly but firmly replied. "When the King told you to look carefully at what's coming out of the mouth, He was also referring to your mouth."

"NO, HE WASN'T," the Mayor screamed out as he walked away. One of the reasons why he was so mad was he realized that sooner or later everyone would have to move off the island unless the spring cleared up.

Early the next day, a huge ship was spotted as it was heading toward the island in the morning fog.

"The enemy is attacking," Mayor Saved Soul shouted to the guards gathered around him on the Beach of Mind. He was looking through his binoculars at the large ship coming his way. "Resist the enemy," the Mayor ordered. All the guards shot in the direction of the ship with their resistant rifles. The ship kept its distance, staying just outside range of the resistant bullets. After a while, it sailed away, as the guards and the Mayor shouted for joy. The joy was short-lived, however. Reality was sinking into everyone's heart. A few more days without water and everyone would be forced to evacuate their beloved island.

The ship returned the next day, but the Mayor and his thirsty guards were ready for it. This time there was no fog around. "Whose ship is it?" the Mayor asked his commanding guard who was examining it with the binoculars.

"Mayor...Dee...Livered," he answered flatly as he read the name on the side of the ship.

"Such a wicked man!" the Mayor yelled. "Taking advantage of us in our time of weakness! I'll die before I let him take over my island!"

On the third day the ship returned once again. The Mayor wasn't down at the beach this time. He was home sick, suffering from severe dehydration. He was so weak that he was unable to get up out of bed. There was no clean water anywhere on the island to drink, but he was too stubborn to leave. "Why didn't the King help me?" the Mayor said to himself. "He said He'd help me. What's he waiting for?"

Down at the beach the guards were also feeling the effects of having no water to drink. They were almost too tired to stand. "Resist them," the commanding guard bravely instructed the other guards, echoing his Mayor's orders. This time, when the ship got close to the island, a small boat was lowered to the water, and a man jumped in. He proceeded to load jug after jug of fresh, spring water into the boat. He then held up a white flag and kept waving it as a sign of peace as the boat got closer and closer to land. By strict orders of the Mayor, they shot ferociously at the enemy ship. The boat was swiftly coming within range of their resistance bullets.

"That guy must be crazy," the commanding guard thought. "He's sure to die, but he doesn't seem to care."

Even over the sound of gunfire everyone could faintly hear the man in the boat screaming something. "Water...I have water for you...I come in peace... Water, I have water for you."

Suddenly the commanding guard screamed out, "Hold your fire! Everybody, hold your fire!"

Loud and clear, the man in the boat could now be easily heard saying, "I come in peace. I have water for you. I come from Mayor Dee Livered with fresh water for you all."

The guards couldn't believe it! Fresh water? And from Mayor Dee Livered, of all people! Everyone knew how wicked Mayor Dee Livered was. How could such a wicked man be so kind as to send water? It must be a trap!

"Guards, prepare to shoot on command," the commanding guard shouted. What a strange sight! A lone man in a small boat making his way to the Beach of Mind, as hundreds of guards stood their ground; all of them pointing their rifles right at him. Certainly, he was either very brave, or very crazy. He came ashore, holding a jug of water in each hand and walked up to the commanding guard.

"My name is Mr. Helpful. I'm Mayor Dee Livered's personal assistant," he said, panting for breath. "A while ago Mayor Dee Livered received word from King Jesus to send water to your island. I've been trying to get this to you for days." He placed the jugs on the sand and turned around and went back to his boat. He came back with two more jugs, and then two more, and two more.

"Our entire ship is loaded with water for you," he announced to the dumbfounded, commanding guard. "This should last you about a month. If you need more, just let us know."

The commanding guard cautiously lifted up one of the jugs and carefully sniffed it. It smelled okay. He poured a little on his finger and tasted it. It tasted fine. Then he placed the jug to his mouth and drank about a half a gallon in a few seconds. "This water tastes great!" he yelled. The guards dropped their rifles and ran to the jugs. All of them were extremely thirsty, so they immediately emptied the water into their grateful stomachs. The commanding guard then gave orders to the troops to assist Mr. Helpful in unloading the ship. He shook his hand in gratitude saying, "I'm going to take a few jugs to Mayor Saved Soul. I hope it's not too late. He's dying of dehydration. Hopefully, I'll be back to escort you to his house this evening."

When he arrived at the Mayor's house, Mr. Comforter answered the door. "He won't talk with me," Mr. Comforter said. "Whenever he gets mad at the King, he refuses to speak to me also." After the guard explained the situation, Mr. Comforter instructed, "Go ahead into his room. But don't tell him where you got the water from, or he won't drink it."

The guard walked down the hallway with a glass of water in one hand and a jug with more water in the other. He stopped at the bedroom entrance and listened to the Mayor's voice behind the door. "King Jesus didn't help me. I cried out to Him and he didn't answer. I'm so thirsty. I'm so tired. Why didn't you help me, King Jesus?" the Mayor cried out in agony of soul. His voice was so pathetic it made the tall, strong guard begin to cry.

"Go away, Mr. Comforter," the Mayor yelled to the door as he heard the sniffling. "I don't want to talk to you."

The Commander slowly cracked opened the door. He noticed that streams of tears were running down the Mayor's pitiful face. "Mayor Saved Soul," the guard gently began, "I have water for you, from the King!"

"What? Oh, thank God," the Mayor exclaimed as he lifted himself up and grabbed the glass of water the guard brought over to him. As soon as it was empty, the guard refilled it, again and again. The Mayor's spirit, which had been so downcast, immediately began to revive. He looked out the window and noticed the sun was shining brightly. Thinking out loud, the Mayor said, "Why did it take so long? Why didn't the King send help sooner?"

"I think the messenger who brought the water will be able to answer those questions, sir," the guard said. "He's down at the beach helping the other guards unload an entire ship that's filled with jugs of water like this one!" He quickly continued, not giving the Mayor a chance to comment or ask any probing questions about where the water came from. "I'll bring him here for dinner this evening, sir. We'll be back around six." With that he zipped out of the room.

Mr. Comforter gladly prepared an elaborate dinner for four: the Mayor, the special guest, the Mayor's commanding guard and himself. When they sat down to eat, the questions began. "How big is your ship? How much water did you bring? Did the King send you?"

"Yes," the guest said. "Well, indirectly. The King told my mayor and he sent me."

"And who is your mayor?"

"Mayor Dee Livered, of course. Don't you know?"

"Mayor Dee Livered?" the Mayor screamed as he jumped to his feet. "Mayor Dee Livered! You tell him I don't want his wicked water." And with that, he actually threw his glass of water at his surprised guest.

Some of the water hit Mr. Helpful in the face, as the glass fell to the floor and shattered. Mr. Helpful quietly picked up his napkin and wiped his face off. He didn't say anything for a moment. They he calmly replied, "My dear friend, why did you call the water wicked?"

"Everyone knows your mayor is a scoundrel, a criminal, and he was even unfaithful to his wife!" he yelled back.

"Mayor Saved Soul, you are somehow terribly mistaken. Our mayor is one of the godliest men I know. He and his wife have an excellent marriage.

He is respected by everyone who knows him." Mr. Helpful breathed a deep sigh and then continued. "I did hear that there were a lot of false rumors and gossip about him coming from somewhere. It looks like it's coming from here."

"It's not gossip," the angry, defensive Mayor shot back. "It's the truth, and it didn't originate from me. It came directly from King Jesus. He sent me a personal message, warning us about Mayor Dee Livered. He also told me to have as many people pray about his family problems as I could."

"Mayor Saved Soul, sir, in all due respect, Mayor Dee Livered does not have any family problems. I'm his personal advisor, and I would know. That could not have been a message from the King. It must have been a message from hell, instead."

The Mayor then began to recall all the events of the fateful day of his anniversary dinner. He turned and asked his commanding guard if any enemy ships had attempted to enter the island from the Ocean of Hell the day of the anniversary.

"No sir," he replied. They all sat there in silence for a moment, straining their memories. "Wait a minute," the Commander said. "I do remember hearing an explosion from the area near the Ocean of Hell. I also remember seeing Mrs. Tender Mercy and her niece walking along the shore right around that time. Perhaps they saw something. Has Mrs. Tender Mercy evacuated the island yet?"

Mayor Saved Soul blurted out, "She would die before she'd ever leave Christian Island."

Everyone looked at each other in horror, as the truth of those words sank in. They jumped up from the table, grabbed some water jugs and all ran non-stop to Mrs. Tender Mercy's little cottage. As they entered, they saw her lying on the living room couch, with her cat at her feet. They both were near death, not having had anything to drink for many days.

The Mayor filled a glass, ran over to Mrs. Tender Mercy, lifted her up and put it to her mouth. "Here, Mrs. Mercy, drink this." She was trying to say something, not wanting to drink before she said what she had to say. The Mayor lowered the glass as she whispered, "Cat...first. My cat...first. She's...about to die."

"Okay, okay," the Mayor said as he filled the cat's bowl and carried her over to it. He ran back to Mrs. Tender Mercy and gave her the rest of the glass of water.

A half hour later, the four men sat around the kitchen table as Mrs. Tender Mercy prepared a fragrant stew on the stove. As she cut up onions, garlic, and vegetables, she told them about the day of the banquet.

"My niece and I were walking down the shoreline when all of a sudden we heard a huge explosion in the distance. It sounded like it was coming from deep within the Ocean of Hell. It really startled us. We ran off the beach and looked back to see what had happened."

"What did you see?" Mr. Helper quickly asked.

"We saw what looked like a huge tidal wave, coming from the Ocean; but as it got closer to the shore it just turned into an extra large wave."

"That was it?" the Mayor asked.

"Well, I guess," Mrs. Tender Mercy answered. "But my niece noticed something unusual. There was a corked bottle that seemed to be riding the wave. As it neared the shore, it crashed against the rocks and broke."

"Was there any message in it?" someone asked.

"I'm not sure," she continued. "The bottle was empty, but there seemed to be...snake tracks coming out from the broken glass. The snake was no where in sight, but we did notice a little hole in the sand. It was very peculiar."

"Very peculiar, indeed," Mr. Helper exclaimed. "A message bottle with a snake in it, coming from the Ocean of Hell!"

"Could a snake from Hell possibly disguise himself as an angel from heaven?" the Mayor asked as he began to piece together the puzzling events of the past few months.

"Most certainly," Mrs. Tender Mercy said, as she wiped her hands on her apron and proceeded to thumb through a nearby book. "The Book of King Jesus teaches us that satan is able to transform himself into an angel of light." (2 Corinthians 11:14)

The Mayor then spoke up, speaking very slowly and soberly. "An angel came to me that day with a message, which I thought was from King Jesus. The message said that Mayor Dee Livered was having serious family problems and that I was to get as many people as I could to pray for him."

"That was definitely a message from hell!" Mr. Helper concluded.

The Mayor's commanding guard, who had been on patrol at the beach that day then said, "If it was a message from hell, it wouldn't have been signed as from King Jesus Christ. The enemy hates that name so much that he's unable to even write it without going berserk. Was it signed as simply 'the King' or as 'King Jesus Christ?'"

"I don't remember," the Mayor said in embarrassment, wondering if all the responsibility for the crisis they were in would soon fall upon his shoulders. He hesitated to talk about it further, afraid that his ugly, ungodly attitudes would be exposed.

"So what did you do with the message?" Mr. Helper asked the subdued Mayor.

"I read it...out loud...in front of a large crowd," the Mayor said.

"How could you?" Mr. Helper asked. "How could you not realize that it was a message from Hell? No wonder so many people have gotten sick. You're the one who started spreading gossip and slander throughout the land. Where was your discernment?" Mr. Helper demanded.

The Mayor knew where his discernment was that day. It was muffled by his own selfish desire to impress his guests, especially the outspoken bully who had yelled at him the night before.

"Calm down, Mr. Helper," Mrs. Tender Mercy politely interjected. "What's important now is to figure out what to do to bring healing to this island."

"You're right," Mr. Helper admitted. "I'm sorry, Mayor. Right now, the crucial thing is to find out what happened to that message and also to focus in on how to cleanse your water source from its pollution."

"I think there's a connection between the two," the Mayor reluctantly continued. "After I read the message to the public, it fell...into a hole in the rocks, above the spring."

The commanding guard, who knew the area of the spring well, was very suspicious. "How did the scroll fall from the balcony of the restaurant to the top of the rocks from where the spring flows out of?"

There was a long silence before the answer came.

"Well, I kicked it," the red-faced Mayor said.

Mr. Helpful just had to speak up again. "Mayor Saved Soul, we want to help you get out of the predicament your island is in. But if we are going to have to pull the truth out of you like a dentist pulls teeth, it's going to waste a lot of precious time."

The Mayor jumped to his feet and marched out of the cottage in anger. Mr. Comforter soon caught up with him and walked beside him without speaking. About halfway home, the Mayor finally stopped and blurted out, "Well, I held my tongue, didn't I? I was slow to speak, wasn't I? I didn't say what I wanted to say to that prying, self-appointed detective!"

Mr. Comforter didn't reply, but he was thinking what everyone else in the cottage was thinking, but not voicing out loud. The Mayor would have to go through a lot more breaking before he would be as willing as he needed to be to face his mistakes.

NINE

The next day there was a skeleton crew of guards watching the Beach of Mind. The threat of danger from the outside was minimum compared to the poison coming from within. The black specks in the water were now visibly flowing out from the spring in the heart of the island. The guards were evacuating everyone left on Christian Island, getting ready to blast the rocks off the top of the spring so they could hopefully get the wicked scroll out. A few minutes past noon the blasting began.

The Mayor was sitting at his desk in his office. Right at the top of the hour the phone rang. He lifted up the receiver to hear the voice of his old friend, Mr. Joy. "How are you, dear Mayor Saved Soul?"

"I'm okay."

"Mayor, I've been standing up for you a lot lately."

"What do you mean?" the Mayor nervously asked.

"Everywhere I go, I hear people telling me that the vicious rumors about Mayor Dee Livered actually started with you, there on Christian Island."

Suddenly a loud explosion rocked the heart of the island, just as the pain hit the Mayor's heart. "So, people are saying evil things about me, huh," the Mayor said as he held back the tears and pushed against his chest to try to alleviate the pain.

"Tell me it isn't true, Mayor. The unclean water on Christian Island isn't coming from a spring filled with the sin of gossip, is it?"

"Mr. Joy, I have someone waiting in my office to see me. I have to be going. I'll call you back later. Good-bye."

The phone immediately rang again. Another call from another friend. Another explosion of dynamite. The Mayor put the phone off the hook and slowly rose to his feet, looking out the window as he pushed his hands against his pain-filled chest. He glanced over towards the heart of the island where the explosions were coming from. He also was looking at the stairway of faith that goes from the heart up to the throne of grace where the King dwells. "I should go and see the King," the Mayor said to himself. "I don't know. He'll probably jump on my case just like everyone else is doing." The Mayor started out of his office, quietly making his way through the reception area. Mr. Comforter was silently sitting there, waiting.

"What are you doing here?" the Mayor asked him rather awkwardly.

"Waiting. I was hoping that I could get you to walk to the throne room with me today."

"Not today," the Mayor uttered. "I'm having terrible chest pains. I'm going to bed to get some rest," he said as he rudely walked past him.

"Mayor Saved Soul, if your heart has gotten so hard that you can lie on the phone to Mr. Joy about having an appointment to go to, don't you think it's time to go see the King?"

The Mayor hung down his head in partial repentance, and partial anger. Mr. Comforter put his arm around him and continued. "You know I'm your friend and all I want to do is help you."

"About the only friend I have left, it looks like," the Mayor said, feeling very sorry for himself. "It seems that everyone is spreading rumors about me, now."

"At least these rumors are accurate," Mr. Comforter said.

"Look," the Mayor seriously replied, "most of the people have moved away. Now the heart of the island has been evacuated, and is being blasted to pieces. Don't you think the King is allowing too much to happen to me? How much can a person take?"

"Let's go talk it over with Him."

"No. Not now. Maybe tomorrow."

"Then let me leave you with a message that is clearly from Him," Mr. Comforter said, pulling out the Book of King Jesus. He opened it up and read it to the Mayor. "My son, do not despise the chastening of the Lord, nor be discouraged when you are rebuked by Him. For whom the Lord loves He chastens, and scourges every son whom He receives...that we may be partakers of His holiness." (Hebrews 12:5,6,10) He lowered the Book and then said one simple, little, profound comment before walking away. "With some people...it takes a lot of chastening before their tongues begin to become partakers of the King's holiness."

TEN

The next day the Mayor woke up to the sound of birds singing in the crisp air. "Ah, no more blasting," he thought. "They must have finished last night." As the Mayor was in the kitchen putting butter on his hot toast, he heard someone knocking on the front door. It was the commanding guard.

"Sir, I have terrible news for you," he began. "We were unable to blast through to the bottom of the spring. I'm afraid it's still polluted. The rocks are just too hard. There's nothing more we can do. Also, we're just about out of the water Mayor Dee Livered sent us. If we don't get a fresh supply in the next day or two, I'm going to have to go to another island, perhaps even permanently. I'm not the only guard who feels this way either, sir. Without clean water, we're going to die if we stay here."

"I understand," the Mayor said. "Thanks for doing all you could do. I appreciate it."

He closed the door and went back into the kitchen and sat down and cried. "Let's go to the King," Mr. Comforter said as he entered the room.

"Arc you kidding," the Mayor answered. "I've got something more important to do right now. I've got to call Mayor Dee Livered and ask for another supply of water before everyone leaves me." He pulled himself together and put on his friendliest voice as he dialed Mr. Dee Livered's number. A sweet, friendly voice answered on the other end. "Mrs. Dee Livered, this is Mayor Saved Soul of Christian Island. Can I please speak to your husband?"

"I'm sorry," she began, "but my husband has gone to the mainland of Mammon for a few weeks. Hopefully, he'll be back by the first of next month. Is there anything I can do for you?"

"Did he go on his large ship?"

"We only have one ship, Mayor. And yes, he went by ship."

The upset Mayor quickly thought to himself, "Why did he go to the Mainland? Didn't he realize we would soon need a new supply of water?" He then brazenly asked Mrs. Dee Livered, "What's he doing in Mammon?"

"Well," Mrs. Dee Livered began, searching for the right words. "Well, I wasn't going to say, but since you asked...all the untrue rumors about my husband have spread throughout this entire region. Our tourism business has really been hurt because of it. Since most of the economy of our island depends on tourism, my husband has had to go to work in the coal mines on the mainland. It's the only place that would hire him," she concluded, sniffling slightly as she fought back the tears.

"I see," the Mayor said. "Please tell your husband to call me when he gets home. Good-bye," he said as he slowly put the receiver down on the hook.

The Mayor looked out the window, realizing

that the last remaining guards were leaving their posts on the beach and making their way on board ships and small boats waiting for them on the shore.

"At least they told me they were going to desert me," the depressed Mayor said as he thought about the fact that the few remaining guards were actually evacuating the island. He then spent the entire day calling every mayor he knew, asking for a week's supply of water. People either weren't home or didn't have any boats available to help him.

As the sun was about to go down, the Mayor went out to the scenic overlook behind his residence. From there he could see most of the island, as well as the Beach of Mind in the far distance. He realized that he, Mr. Comforter, and perhaps Mrs. Tender Mercy were the only ones left on the entire island. He fell down to the ground and cried out to the King, "Dear Lord, have mercy on me. I don't want to leave this island. There's nowhere for me to go, except back to the land of Mammon where I was born. I don't want to go back to the world. I don't want to go to a place where Mr. Comforter isn't welcomed; where there's no stairways of faith, nor mercy from heaven. Please, deliver me!" He cried and cried and cried.

Looking up, he noticed the sky was colored with bright reds, purples and oranges, displaying the glory and majesty of its Creator. "King Jesus, if You can make such a lovely sunset, surely you can create in me a clean heart."

Then he heard it. It sounded like the roar of a huge, but friendly lion. The King was speaking from His throne to the Mayor. "MY SON, DESPISE NOT THE CHASTENING OF THE LORD. SUBMIT TO MY CHASTENING HAND, IN FAITH AND TRUST, KNOWING THAT IT IS FOR YOUR GOOD, AND NOT FOR YOUR DESTRUCTION."

The island literally shook at the sound of His voice. It wasn't a terrifying shake, however, but a comforting one. A shake that let the Mayor know the powerful King was able to deliver him.

"Lord, I submit. Do whatever you have to do in order to cleanse out the spring in this, Your island."

The Mayor rose to his feet, somehow knowing that prayer was what the King was waiting for. He expected an army of angels to appear and deliver him. But nothing came, nothing but the appearance of a small cloud in the eastern sky, about the size of a man's hand. The Mayor stood transfixed, looking at the deep blue cloud, amazed at how fast it was growing. Mr. Comforter ran up to the Mayor and grabbed his hand. "Hurry," he exclaimed. "Let's get back to the house while we still can. That cloud is none other than the mighty hand of the Lord's chastening. Let's run for it."

As they began to scurry back to the house, the wind started blowing with extreme intensity. About halfway to the back door the sky started pouring down sheets of water. The rain hit the Mayor so hard he fell to the ground and slid in the mud. Mr. Comforter grabbed his friend and led him the rest of the way. The Mayor was so covered with mud that he couldn't even see in front of him. Right as they entered the door, the wind picked up in intensity and howled like the sound of a mighty freight train.

When they closed the door behind them, they proceeded to wipe the mud off the Mayor's face. As they were doing so, they noticed a sweet smell coming from the kitchen. Mrs. Tender Mercy was preparing dinner! "It's a good thing I decided to come over this evening," she said as her friends entered the kitchen and sat down. "This storm is surely going to flood my little cottage. I've experienced these types of tempests before. This entire island might be flooded before it's over."

Mrs. Tender Mercy was right. The rain lasted through the night, and the next day, and the next night. On the second day the Mayor noticed out the window that almost the entire island was covered with water. Another day or two and the Mayor's house would be flooded with the water of God's chastisement.

During those long, dreary days there wasn't much to do but wait out the storm, and think; think about the events that had happened on Christian Island. One long afternoon the Mayor went to his study and sat down at his desk. As he stared at the now useless phone, he couldn't help remembering the sweet sounding voice of Mayor Dee Livered's wife.

"What a nice lady she is," the Mayor thought. "And I gossiped about her and her husband to everyone who would listen to me! It's certain that Mrs. Dee Livered knew that I was the one who began the vicious gossip about her and her husband. If I were her," he said to himself, "I would have screamed at whoever gossiped about me. My heart really has been growing hard. My mouth has caused so much damage, not only to this island, but also to Mayor Dee Livered's life as well." He opened a desk drawer and pulled out the scroll Mr. Comforter had given him many weeks before. "I really do need to learn these truths," he thought, as he opened the scroll and began to read:

"Let every man be swift to hear, slow to speak, slow to wrath; for the wrath of man does not produce the righteousness of God.

If anyone among you thinks he is religious, and does not bridle his tongue but deceives his own heart, this one's religion is useless.

The tongue is a fire, a world of iniquity. The tongue is so set among our members that it defiles our whole body, and sets on fire the course of nature; and it is set on fire by hell. For every kind of beast and bird, of reptile and creature of the sea, is tamed and has been tamed by mankind. But no man can tame the tongue. It is an unruly evil, full of deadly poison. With it we bless our God and Father, and with it we curse men, who have been made in the similitude of God. Out of the same mouth proceed blessing and cursing. My brethren, these things ought not so to be. Does a spring send forth fresh water and bitter water from the same opening?

Do not speak evil of one another, brethren. He who speaks evil of a brother and judges his brother, speaks evil of the law and judges the law. But if you judge the law, you are not a doer of the law but a judge. There is one lawgiver, who is able to save and destroy. Who are you to judge another? Do not grumble against one another, brethren, lest you be condemned. Behold, the Judge is standing at the door. " (James 1:19-20,26, 3:6-11, 4:11-12, 5:9 NKJV)

The more he read, the more he cried. He reread the contents of the scroll over and over again. Finally, he fell to his knees and began to really pray, with all his heart. "Dear King Jesus, forgive me for the sins of my mouth. If I hadn't of wanted to impress those guests, I would have realized the message about Mayor Dee Livered wasn't from You. Forgive me for spreading gossip and slander about him and his wife. Forgive me for being so hard-hearted and stubborn, and not caring about all the people I've hurt with my tongue. Cleanse my heart, Lord. Cleanse my soul. Cleanse my tongue." He stayed on his knees for a long time and wept as he poured out his soul. He then felt the forgiving, cleansing love of God flowing through his heart. He arose to his feet, knowing that he was surely forgiven and truly cleansed. "Once this trial is over, with God's help, I'm never going to spread rumors about anyone, ever again," he determined.

When he walked into the kitchen, he overheard Mr. Comforter and Mrs. Tender Mercy whispering. "Do you realize this house is about to collapse under the weight of this storm?" Mrs. Tender Mercy said to Mr. Comforter. When they noticed the Mayor, they wondered how he'd react to a statement that he may not want to hear.

"I've placed my heart into the Lord's hands," the broken Mayor declared. "It's totally up to Him as to how long this trial will last. And if this house collapses--yet I will trust in Him. I've determined to never again speak evil of any person; and that most certainly includes my King. Never again will I murmur about His dealings. He does all things well," the Mayor said with a confidence and repentance that came from the depths of his heart and soul.

As the word "well" left his mouth a loud bolt of lightning thundered down from heaven into the heart of the island. The impact caused the house to be lifted up into the air a few feet and then it came crashing down. All three of them were thrown to the floor, as pieces of the ceiling tile fell down upon them. The Mayor closed his eyes, thinking that death was a moment away. "Thank God I got right with the Lord before I died," he thought. But he didn't die. He wasn't even scratched. None of them were hurt, although no one was in a hurry to get up, or even move.

They laid there on the ground for five or six

minutes, quietly listening to the sounds of the massive storm outside. In a matter of minutes the storm died down, and then the rain stopped as suddenly as it had begun. As they were helping each other up, they noticed the welcomed sunshine was breaking through the clouds and coming through the kitchen window.

"The storm of God's chastisement is over," Mr. Comforter announced with a deep sigh of relief.

"Even if it isn't, its okay with me," the changed Mayor said.

"That's precisely why it's over," Mrs. Tender Mercy said with a smile.

The Mayor didn't quite understand what that meant, but he would figure it out later. Now he had to go outside and check on the condition of the island. He ran out to the overlook, and what a sight he saw! Everything in sight had been flooded. The water was quickly receding back to the ocean as the island emerged like a toy duck being carefully lifted out of a bathtub. A soaked island arose from the ocean in a matter of seconds. The Mayor was amazed. "Wow," he yelled out as he realized what was happening. The hand of God that plunged the whole island into an Ocean of Affliction had lifted it out of it in a moment of time. "What a mighty God you are, King Jesus!" As he spoke those words, the stairway of faith rose to the heavens from the heart of the island. Mr. Comforter was now at his side. "Let's go worship the King, at His footstool," Mr. Comforter suggested.

"Sounds great to me," he said with a happy smile.

As they walked to the heart of the island, Mr. Comforter purposely took the Mayor past the spring. The rocks were still smoking from the blast of God's lightning bolt that had split them apart at the end of the storm. The Mayor walked to the top of the spring and looked inside the hole. There at the bottom, was the corroded, demonic scroll. The Mayor reached down and grabbed it. It was now a black piece of corrosion, a wilted snake skin. As he attempted to open it up, it crumbled to pieces and fell back into the water. In a few minutes the fresh water from the spring washed the pollution out into the river going to the ocean. "The spring is clean again!" the Mayor said triumphantly. "Praise the living God for His mercy and grace." The Mayor and his assistant walked up the stairway of faith, singing all the way, "Praise the living God, for His mercy and His grace! We love to come to Him; we love to seek His face!" As nothing but pure praise flowed out of the Mayor's mouth, nothing but pure, wholesome, fresh spring water flowed out from the spring into the entire island.

CONCLUSION

"My dear Savior," the Mayor said as he ran into the King's waiting arms. "This was such a hard lesson to learn," he said as rested in his Lord's strong arms. "I hope the spring never becomes contaminated, ever again," he said as he sat down on the steps surrounding the Lord's throne. The King sat down upon His throne and lovingly looked down at His feet where the Mayor was sitting. "Before you repair the houses on the island that have been damaged by the storm, can I make a suggestion?"

"By all means," the Mayor exclaimed, chuckling inside at the thought that the King of Kings was asking a little Mayor like himself permission to do something.

"The first thing you need to build is a fence around the mouth of the spring. It will serve as a protection against any scrolls of gossip or slander ever falling into it in the future."

"That's a great idea!" the Mayor replied. "As a matter of fact, I'm going to build a tall, rock wall around it. And I'm going to set a guard over the mouth, to make sure no one even tries to climb over it. That will keep any corrupt thing from ever again proceeding out of the mouth of Christian Island."

"Concerning your statement about learning lessons the hard way," the King continued. "I too would prefer you not have to go through such heart-rending trials. Some of the lessons of life can be learned in a much easier fashion."

"And how is that?" the humbled Mayor asked.

"If you would only listen more carefully to Mr. Comforter. I've sent him into your life to be your personal assistant. He's a gift to you from My Father and I. He walks with you and talks with you wherever you go. He's always there, and always ready to give you My words and guide you into My ways. Don't grieve him, and don't quench him, and by all means don't ignore him. Be very attentive to His voice and you will be able to learn life's lessons a lot easier, and a lot faster."

The Mayor remembered all the times that Mr. Comforter tried to speak to his stubborn heart. He clearly recalled that many weeks ago his assistant gave him the scroll filled with insights about the sin of gossip and slander. "Yes," the Mayor thoughtfully acknowledged, "I do need to diligently guard my mouth, and I also must definitely listen more carefully to Mr. Comforter."

BOOK THREE:

Healing From The Disease Of Discontentment

INTRODUCTION TO BOOK THREE

Have you ever noticed how rare it is to find people that we can honestly describe as deeply content? Discontentment surely is rampant in our fallen world. Is it any wonder? Mankind, created in the very image and likeness of Almighty God, made for the purpose of communing with his amazing Creator, is trying to satisfy his soul with petty, trivial pursuits. King Solomon knew from experience that, "He that loveth silver shall not be satisfied with silver; nor he that loveth abundance with increase." (Ecclesiastes 5:10)

In the following parable, Mayor Saved Soul of Christian Island takes long detours on his journey to the place of contentment. His lengthy struggle reminds us that this "disease" doesn't just plague the unsaved. Even among believers there are strong tendencies for us to try to find satisfaction in all the wrong places. Paul, the Apostle admonished Timothy with these words: "Contentment with godliness is great gain...having food and clothing, let us be content." (1 Timothy 6:6,8 NKJV) He told the Philippians, "I have learned in whatever state I am in to be content." (4:8 NKJV) The Word of God clearly teaches us that Christ, not things, is to be our source of contentment: "Let your conduct be without covetousness, and be content with such things as you have. For He, Himself (Jesus) has said, 'I will never leave you, nor forsake

137

you.'" (Hebrews 13:5 NKJV)

A prophetic word spoken through Jeremiah centuries ago holds a key for God's people today who are searching for deep and lasting contentment. "The Lord has redeemed Jacob, and ransomed him from the hand of one stronger than he. Therefore they shall come and sing in the height of Zion, streaming to the goodness of the Lord...and My people shall be satisfied with My goodness, says the Lord." (Jeremiah 31:11,12,14b)

ONE

In the Sea of Humanity, off the coast of Mammon, there's an island called Christian, where Mr. Saved Soul is the Mayor. Because of the presence of God that permeated the land, Mayor Saved Soul was a very blessed man.

One spring morning, the Mayor woke up unusually early, in an exceptionally good mood. He decided to spend some extra time with his Lord that day. It was his custom to take at least two daily walks up to the golden throne room; first thing in the morning and before retiring in the evening. His faithful companion, Mr. Comforter, was always available to assist him on these short, but vital journeys.

The stars were still shining brightly in the pre-dawn sky as he left his home and began walking towards the heart of Christian Island. The eastern horizon was just beginning to turn light blue, while crickets were still chirping in the serene, night air. As the Mayor approached the center of the island, Mr. Comforter quietly joined him. They both marveled at the beauty of the stairway of faith that ascended into the sky ahead of them. It had a soft, magnificent glow to it. The glory from the golden throne room was flowing down upon it like the mist from a large, fluorescent waterfall. What a refreshing mist it was! As they walked through the corridor of conscience and onto the first steps, they both felt stronger and lighter.

Halfway up the stairway they stopped for a moment and looked down on the sleepy island. They could see lights popping on throughout the land as the inhabitants were awakening to a promising, new day.

"What a fortunate person I am," the grateful Mayor said to his assistant as they continued up the steps. "I have a beautiful home, good health, and plenty of faithful, wonderful friends, such as yourself. To top it all off, I have access to the throne room of King Jesus twenty-four hours a day, seven days a week!" The Mayor then walked into the golden room, holding his breath like a happy child being thrown into a swimming pool in mid-August, as the majesty of God's glory fell upon him. He soon got on his knees and then on his face as he delightfully found himself swept up into singing the everlasting song of the Lamb that was resounding around the throne. "Worthy is the Lamb that was slain, Worthy Is The Lamb That Was Slain, WORTHY IS THE LAMB THAT WAS SLAIN!" There was a mixture of angelic and human voices, accompanied by harps, violins, flutes, and various other instruments.

The Mayor was about to get totally caught up in worship when his mind began to remember all the many things he had scheduled for the day. "Let's see, I need to go to the post office, and then the grocery store. Then I need to visit so and so. And, oh yes, I have a luncheon appointment at eleven-thirty." He was still lying on the floor of the throne room, but he was no longer hearing or joining in with the heavenly worshipers. Instead, he was wondering if he had enough time to get everything done. He quietly got up and walked out of the room and slowly headed down the stairway. By this time the morning sun was brightly shining on the dew, causing it to sparkle on the grass throughout the island. "It's so wonderful to be alive," the Mayor exclaimed to Mr. Comforter as they walked down into the heart of the island together.

Mr. Comforter replied, "Yes, it sure is. And Mayor, you don't have to be so concerned about getting everything done in one day. Whatever you don't have time to do can just wait till the next day. Right?" he asked with a smile.

"Right," the Mayor said. "Why don't you head on home and start breakfast. I'll be there in a little while. I'll save some time if I stop off at the post office on the way."

Mr. Comforter nodded his head, and walked away, wondering if the Mayor had even heard his wise council.

TWO

In a few, short minutes, the Mayor opened his post office box, and noticed that there was a ton of junk mail along with one personal letter for him. "From Mayor Ree Deemed! I haven't heard from him in ages! I wonder how he's doing," he said to himself as he quickly tore open the envelope.

"Dear Mayor Saved Soul," he read as he walked out of the post office, "I sure hope all is well with you. I'd love to have you over for lunch this Saturday the tenth, at noon. If I don't hear otherwise, I'll be expecting you. Sincerely, Mayor Ree Deemed." He stuffed the letter into his pocket and headed home. "Saturday, the tenth! That's tomorrow! Good thing I got up early today. I have a million things to get done in order to take off tomorrow afternoon." He rushed home so he could hurry up and eat and have time to do all the things on his already busy schedule.

THREE

The next morning the Mayor woke up late. He didn't get enough sleep because he stayed up half the night before. "I'll have to hurry if I'm going to make it to the throne room this morning," the Mayor yelled out to Mr. Comforter as he quickly gobbled down a muffin and some juice. He then jogged to the throne room, not because he needed the exercise, but because the only boat going to Mayor Ree Deemed's island that day was leaving in thirty minutes.

When Mr. Comforter walked into the golden throne room a little while after the Mayor arrived, he saw him sitting on a bench, staring at his watch! "Why are you timing yourself, Mayor?" he politely inquired.

"Because I have to catch the ten o'clock boat," he said as he rose to his feet to leave.

"Where are you going?"

"Oh, I didn't tell you?" the Mayor asked, being a little embarrassed that he forgot to mention his plans to Mr. Comforter. "Mayor Ree Deemed invited me to be his special guest for lunch today. Perhaps I should give him a call and ask if it's okay to bring you along."

"No, that's all right," Mr. Comforter said. "I'll see you this evening when you get back."

FOUR

Mayor Ree Deemed's house was built on a hill near the center of his lovely island. It was very similar to Mayor Saved Soul's, except for one major difference. Its enormous porch encircled the entire front of the house and most of the two sides. The roof of the house extended over it and its glass walls created a spacious, garden feeling, providing a beautiful view of the ocean. A perfect setting to entertain lunch guests. Mayor Ree Deemed was indeed a gracious host. He had a delicious meal prepared for his good friend, which Mayor Saved Soul thoroughly enjoyed. After the meal, the two Mayors spent time catching up on what they had been doing since their last visit.

"I've been spending more and more time with the King lately," Mayor Ree Deemed said with a tone of deep contentment in his voice and a sparkle in his eyes. "What a difference it makes when we spend quality time with God!"

"How long did it take for you to have this porch built?" Mayor Saved Soul asked, as he glanced around the large room.

"Oh, it took way too long," he replied. "I'd say it took me about a month, and..."

"You built it yourself?" Mayor Saved Soul interrupted as he noticing the excellent craftsmanship.

"Yeah," Mayor Ree Deemed answered, without

much enthusiasm. He wanted to talk about King Jesus, but to his dismay, Mayor Saved Soul seemed much more interested in discussing his porch.

Mayor Saved Soul got up and walked over to the windows and carefully placed his right hand against the glass. "How did you connect these windows together?" he asked as he thought about the possibility of building his own enclosed porch.

"I connected them at the top," he said, pointing to the ceiling. Giving in to the way the conversation was going, Mayor Ree Deemed reluctantly asked, "Would you like for me to give you a tour of the porch?"

"Sure," the Mayor exclaimed. "And, do you have any paper, and a pencil?"

Mayor Ree Deemed took his friend outside and showed him how he laid the foundation, extended the ceiling and built the walls of the porch. "Let's go have some tea before you leave," Mayor Ree Deemed suggested, heading back inside. He turned around, noticing the occupied Mayor wasn't following him. "I'll be right there," the Mayor said as he briskly scratched out a diagram of the porch's foundation.

As they were sipping tea, Mayor Ree Deemed shared various incidents in his personal life and the life of his island. Mayor Saved Soul was only half listening, however. He was thinking about how to lighten his schedule enough to build his own enclosed front porch. He thought to himself, "I probably have enough wood in my basement to build a balcony onto the front of my house. That means I'd only have to buy the glass! Perhaps Mr. Comforter would be willing to help me."

Mayor Ree Deemed asked the daydreaming Mayor, "So, when does your boat head back to Christian Island?"

"Uh, yeah," the Mayor said, trying not to give the impression that he wasn't listening. "Yeah, I'm taking the boat back today."

"When does it leave?" Mayor Ree Deemed patiently asked again.

"It leaves at two-thirty," the Mayor said. "Oh my," he gasped as he looked down at his watch. "It's two-twenty! I've gotta run. Thanks for the great lunch. I'll keep in touch." He ran down to the beach and got to the boat just as it was about to head out of the dock. As he found a seat, he pulled out his sketches and began to plan in his mind how he would build his own beautiful, front porch.

FIVE

The next few days Mayor Saved Soul worked at a frantic pace. He would promptly get done with his duties and then spend the rest of the afternoon and evening shut up in his office. His desk top was covered with an extra large sketch pad he recently bought. He scribbled and scribbled, erased and scribbled for hours. He made drawings of how the balcony would look from every angle. When he got a particular drawing just right, he would sketch it on a clean sheet of paper. Right when he was just about finished with the last drawing, Mr. Comforter walked in and looked over his shoulder at his work.

"What do you think?" the Mayor asked with such enthusiasm that the question almost demanded a positive response.

"I think the back porch is sufficient," Mr. Comforter bluntly answered.

"But it wouldn't take much money. I can build it myself, and it would only cost the price of the materials. That wouldn't be a lot because I think I already have enough wood in the basement."

Mr. Comforter could tell from the tone of his voice that the Mayor's mind was already made up. He was going to build his porch, regardless of how much cold water anyone would try to throw on his plans.

"Well," Mr. Comforter began, "you'd better be very careful when you pull up the weeds in the front yard. There's some poisonous plants growing out there, you know."

"Yes, I know. I'll be sure to wear my garden gloves," the Mayor said with glee, almost jumping for joy as he arose from his chair. He danced around in a circle as he proclaimed, "The view is going to be spectacular! We'll be able to see the ocean from here. We'll have great luncheons. It'll be worth the effort. You'll see."

Mr. Comforter walked away, feeling that trouble was brewing.

SIX

It took nearly two weeks for Mayor Saved Soul to pull up all the stubborn weeds in his front yard, clearing a space for the balcony's foundation. During this time he was careful not to neglect his daily visits to the throne room; but slowly, something was happening to the Mayor. He was there, but he wasn't. He was still having devotions, but his heart wasn't fully in it. His mind was consumed with his little building project. While in the presence of the King, he would still faithfully pray about all his needs and the needs of those around him. He would still sing praises and worship, at least with his mouth. Little by little, however his heart was drawn away to earthly things. While everyone around him was caught up in worship, he would find himself thinking about all the wonderful times he would have on his new, enclosed porch.

SEVEN

One morning the Mayor awoke with intense itching on the inside of his hands and the bottom of his feet. He noticed a few itchy red spots here and there that grew and grew as he scratched them. The next day, the spots increased dramatically in number and size. Soon, they began to appear on his face, also. He diligently went to the King and prayed constantly for his healing. The Mayor would approach the throne and get on his knees with his itchy hands out in front of him. As he prayed, he would stare at the spots that were daily becoming more and more an uncomfortable nuisance. He would convey all his worries and fears to the compassionate King, imploring the Lord to heal him. Emotionally, he would always feel better after he prayed, but physically he got worse and worse. His times in the throne room were no longer filled with worship, praise, and thanksgiving. Only frantic prayer.

Someone advised the Mayor to go see a well-known doctor on the coast of Mammon named Doctor Whiz Dum. "These spots must have been caused from the poisonous weeds in your front yard," this person assumed. "Perhaps the doctor could at least give you something to alleviate the itching while you wait for the King to heal you." So, after prayer one morning, Mayor Saved Soul had an announcement for Mr. Comforter.

"I've got a private errand to run, today. I'll see

you back at the house later this evening."

He didn't want to tell his counselor he was going to see a doctor in the land of Mammon. He knew he wouldn't approve of that. Even the captain of his private boat looked at him with unbelief when he announced, "I need for you to take me to the northern coast of Mammon, as quickly as possible."

EIGHT

Doctor Whiz Dum carefully examined the red spots on the hands and face of the frightened Mayor. "Yes, it's what I was afraid of," the elderly doctor said. "You have a serious case of discontentment. If not carefully and immediately treated, it will only get worse. It could eventually totally incapacitate you. It might even prove to be fatal!"

"But, uh, what do you think caused it, Doc?" the stunned Mayor asked.

"I don't know for sure. What were you doing differently when you first noticed the spots?"

"I was...pulling up poisonous weeds in my front yard," the Mayor answered.

"That must be the cause," the doctor declared, although he was merely guessing.

"What can be done? I'm too young to die! Do I need to change my diet? Should I move to a milder climate? Surely there's something that can be done!"

"Oh, yes," the doctor confidently remarked. "I'm sure we can take care of this problem." He abruptly scratched out something on a prescription pad, and handed the paper to the desperate Mayor. "Here. This ought to do it. If not, come back and see me in a few months and we'll try something else."

The Mayor jumped down from the examining table, reading the prescription out loud, as the doctor suddenly left to go see another waiting patient. "Take continual, heavy doses of excitement."

On the way back to the island, the Mayor's private boat captain also appeared noticeably nervous. Neither one of them talked for most of the return trip. The distraught Mayor just stared out into the ocean, numb and scared. Finally the captain spoke up. "Mayor Saved Soul," he began, "I'm sure you're aware that I won't be able to bring you back to the doctor's for at least four weeks."

The Mayor looked over at him with a blank stare, wondering why this was so, but not really caring why. The captain slowly continued. "My annual trip around the world is coming up. Remember? I take every June off from work and go around the globe for my yearly vacation."

The Mayor didn't reply. The silence was long and tense.

The captain finally asked, "It's okay if I take the month of June off, isn't it, sir?"

"Yes, of course," the Mayor replied.

"Oh, thank you, Mayor! I'm so excited! It's always the highlight of the year for me. It's so exciting to visit other cities and islands and nations and cultures!"

"Mr. Captain?" the Mayor interrupted.

"Yes?" the captain asked, hoping he wasn't about to change his mind about giving him permission to take time off.

"Mr. Captain, can I go with you?"

"Uh, yeah. Sure! Are you serious?"

The Mayor nodded his head, and then broke out with a big smile.

"Oh, this is great!" Mr. Captain yelled. "We'll stop at all the famous ports, see all the attractions, eat at the most famous restaurants in the world!"

The Mayor also started getting really excited. He happened to look down at his hands. "Look," he screamed, "the spots are fading! They're leaving me! I'm getting well! It's working!" By the time the Mayor reached home the spots were almost gone. They had completely disappeared from his face and feet. Only a few small dots remained on the inside of his right hand. The excitement of the upcoming trip was curing the Mayor of his discontentment; temporarily, that is. The Mayor immediately went to the travel agency office on Christian Island and loaded himself up with brochures, maps and magazines. The excitement kept building and he kept feeling better and better.

Mr. Comforter didn't feel good about the trip, though. "But what about your daily visits to the throne room?" he objected.

"I promise, I'll read the Book of King Jesus every day, and I'll be sure to begin the mornings in prayer. I know the Lord wouldn't mind. I'm sure it'll help me get better. Surely He wouldn't object to that, would He?"

NINE

The day to begin their big trip soon arrived. The Mayor took so much luggage that there was no room for Mr. Comforter in the small boat. "I'll see you in about a month," the extremely excited Mayor said as the boat slowly backed out of the dock. "I promise, I'll pray at least thirty minutes every morning," he yelled out to his counselor as the boat's motor propelled them away.

The Mayor did make good on that promise. No matter where they were, no matter how late they would go to sleep, no matter how much was planned for the day ahead, the Mayor faithfully had prayer time each morning, usually for exactly thirty minutes. The half hour seemed like an awfully long time. His mind couldn't help wandering off to the tourist attractions and restaurants and museums that were on the agenda for the day ahead. It truly was one of the most exciting times in the Mayor's life. It was like a whole month of field trips; thirty days of fun and pleasure! The red spots were completely gone, except for two faint spots on the inside of his right hand. Every once in a while, at the height of an exciting moment, the Mayor would inconspicuously open his hand and notice that the spots were still there. In the middle of a great roller-coaster ride, or in the midst of an exquisite dinner, or during an international sports event, he would suddenly check his hand, and always be disappointed to see those pesky, little spots.

"What's the next major port?" the Mayor asked one day.

"That's it, sir," the worn out captain said. "Tomorrow morning...we head home!"

"You mean, it's been a whole month, already? The trip is almost over?" the nervous Mayor anxiously asked.

"Yes," the captain answered. "It's been great, but I'm good and ready to get back to my usual, daily, boring routines."

"I'm feeling a little sick," the Mayor uttered. "Perhaps I'm getting sea-sick. I've got to lie down for a little while."

As the Mayor tossed and turned he looked down at his hands. The two small red dots were quickly growing! In a few hours there were five dots on his hand. The disease appeared to be coming back! It did come back, and with a vengeance. Soon, his right hand was covered with the red rash of discontentment. By the time he arrived home and unpacked his luggage, that hand was in a lot of pain.

The next morning the Mayor walked into the throne room, holding his pain-filled right hand in his other hand. "Dear Lord," he cried out as he fell on his knees before the throne, "please heal me! Please, have mercy on my hand. Please, cure me of this horrible disease I have." He cried and cried and pled and cried for fifteen long minutes.

When he was finished, the King was about to speak to His friend. But before the Lord could say anything, the Mayor abruptly jumped up and nearly ran out of the throne room. The Mayor had suddenly remembered the last words the doctor had told him weeks ago. "Come back and see me if you need to, and we'll try something else."

TEN

Back in Dr. Whiz Dum's office the Mayor poured out his frustrations. "It was great for a while, Doc," the Mayor confided. "The excitement really did take the discontentment away. But on the way home, the rash came back seven times worse. It used to just itch, but now it's also burning and hurting me, terribly."

"Hummm," the doctor responded, scratching his head. He pulled out his prescription pad, scribbled on it, and handed it to the desperate Mayor. It said, "Take heavy, continual doses of achievement."

A few days later the Mayor decided to join an expedition that was about to begin, far away on the mainland of Mammon. He decided to accomplish something he always had a desire to do. He was going to go mountain climbing! Along with a small group of adventurous men, he would try the impossible. In the span of one week they determined to climb the two highest peaks in the land of Mammon, Mt. Fame and Mt. Fortune. Not only was this exciting and thrilling, but it also promised to give a great sense of achievement. The rest of the team had no relationship whatsoever with King Jesus, and their attitudes and words constantly reflected this. Mr. Comforter didn't want any part of such foul-mouthed speech, so he would wait for the Mayor at the base of the mountains.

It took only two days to climb to the top of Mt.

Fame. Although it was a great accomplishment, the Mayor was disappointed with the view from the top. "I actually have a better view from the scenic overlook on my little island," the frustrated Mayor said to himself as he stood on the top of Mt. Fame and looked out across the barren, desolate country of Mammon.

Mt. Fortune was a much steeper climb. Many people had recently lost their lives trying to conquer this treacherous peak. At about the halfway point, two men in the back lost their footing at the same time, and fell a thousand feet into the valley of greed. When another member of their team fell into the ravine of extortion the rest of them were ready to turn back. Mayor Saved Soul, feeling the painful spots inside his hands, cried out, "No! We must make it to the top!"

A few hours later they arrived at their destination. The team pulled out bottles of champagne and made a toast to Mayor Saved Soul, the champion of the expedition. The Mayor didn't join in their drinking, but he sure felt great! What an accomplishment! Not only was he part of a team who broke all previous worldly records, but everyone knew it was the Mayor's stubborn refusal to quit that had made the difference.

When they happily arrived at the bottom of the mountain, crowds of reporters and cameramen were waiting. Instantly, all types of companies and corporations were offering contracts to the climbers to endorse their products. Fame and fortune were being poured out on all of them, but especially on the valiant Mayor. He was the hero of the day! Everyone thought the Mayor refused to quit because he wasn't a quitter, no matter what obstacles would come his way. The truth of the matter was that his determination was fueled by the fact that the red spots on his hand refused to heal. Even as the reporters were asking questions and flashing their cameras the Mayor kept pulling his glove off, secretly looking at the palm of his hand, wondering why those last two stubborn little red dots just wouldn't leave.

When the Mayor reached home, he was surprised to find that his fame had gone on ahead of him. All the area newspapers were loaded with thrilling stories about the famous expedition. Many of the articles were filled with exaggerations and half truths, but the fact could not be denied. Mayor Saved Soul had accomplished a great task, and the people on his little island were naturally proud and happy for him. They put on an elaborate home-coming parade followed by an expensive feast for their beloved Mayor. It was all extremely exciting, and it was sure a heavy dose of achievement for him.

The following morning, on the way to the throne room the Mayor tried to convince Mr. Comforter how worthwhile the expedition was. "That dose of excitement and achievement did me a lot of good. It was an amazing accomplishment! We climbed two major peaks in one week!"

While in the throne room, however, the Mayor lost all desire to tell the King about his "great" accomplishments. In the light of the Lord's holiness and glory everything can be seen in its proper perspective. "My mountain climbing expedition wasn't so fantastic," the Mayor acknowledged to himself. "It didn't help anyone. It didn't prove anything. Actually, come to think of it, it was a shallow achievement, and I'm not totally healed, either," he realized as he looked down at his red-spotted palm. "I know what the solution is," he reasoned. "I need to accomplish great things, for God. Yes! That's how I'll be completely healed. I'll do great things for God," he proclaimed out loud at he walked out of the throne room.

As he was walking down the stairway of faith, he started up a conversation with his counselor, Mr. Comforter. "I'm so excited! I now understand what my calling in life is: to accomplish great things for God!"

"That's wonderful," Mr. Comforter acknowledged. "But what's the motive?"

"I'll see you this evening," the Mayor said, without even addressing that piercingly important question. "I have a great idea I need to look into," he concluded as he briskly walked away, heading toward the island's spring.

Mr. Comforter just stood there, watching Mayor Saved Soul run off to accomplish great things for God. "But what's the motive?" Mr. Comforter quietly echoed into the wind.

ELEVEN

Within a few short months, Mayor Saved Soul built an elaborate water-bottling company at the source of the spring on Christian Island. Since the water was so refreshingly delicious it was an instant success. The business was so profitable that the Mayor was soon able to donate thousands of gallons of water to various other islands. One month he received word that Mayor Dee Livered's water supply had somehow become contaminated. He gladly loaded up his boat with tons of water. He and Mr. Captain sped away to help his needy neighbor, with no questions asked. He continually made trips to that island for as long as it took for the spring to clear up. Mayor Saved Soul felt better than he had for years. He was excited about life, and was so happy that he was accomplishing great things for God! All the spots were fading; all, except for the two little faint spots on the inside of his right hand.

The Mayor decided that he needed to do even more sacrificial things for his Lord and the Lord's people. With the permission of Mr. Captain, he turned his boat into an intercessory warship. Through intercessory prayer the Mayor would come to the defense of people in heavy spiritual conflicts. One morning the Mayor practically ran down to the docks. He jumped into the boat, saying to Mr. Captain, "I heard Mayor Ree Deemed is being attacked by a barge from hell. Let's go and fight for him!" Somewhere near the Ocean of Hell the Mayor's gunboat headed off the huge, demonic barge. The barge was filled with tons of garbage and many wicked demons. In comparison to the Mayor's little gunboat it seemed like a double-decker bus being chased by a puppy. But they were able to hinder the barge for a little while, which was just long enough for Mayor Ree Deemed to get the help he needed from the King.

A wonderful sense of accomplishment settled down upon the Mayor's heart. He had put his very life on the line for the cause of Christ and to help a fellow believer! "Now I'm really living," he began to constantly say to himself. He fought valiantly many times and in many places for other islands who were being attacked by the enemy. Unnoticeably, the Mayor's daily visits with the King slowly started suffering. He was so busy fighting the battles for the Lord that the quality and length of his times with the Lord got less and less. He was on more and more crusades for the God he was spending less and less time with. He still had some wonderful times in the throne room, but they were few and far between. He decided that must be the way it is. He just had to learn to accept it. That also became his attitude about the few red spots still on the palm of his hand. "I guess I'll just have to live with it," he thought to himself. "I'll just make sure I stay busy helping others."

TWELVE

One day, the Mayor went down to the dock to fight spiritual battles for some neighbors in dire need. He noticed that the boat was out of the water, being held up by a large crane. Mr. Captain came over to the puzzled Mayor, saying, "Mayor, I'm so sorry. I hit another boat yesterday while I was backing out of the port. It was so clumsy of me. It caused extensive damage, so I'll have to wait a while till I can save up enough money to get it fixed."

"But, but, we have to get that boat fixed, right away," the Mayor nervously replied as he pulled out his wallet, and frantically counted his money. "How much is it gonna cost?" he asked.

"About five hundred dollars, at least," Mr. Captain said, apologetically.

"Here's a hundred and ten," the Mayor said, emptying his wallet. "I'll get the rest this afternoon, and we'll head out to the ocean tomorrow morning. Okay?" he asked.

"Thank you very much, sir," Mr. Captain said, taking the money and stuffing it in his pocket. "But sir, its still going to take at least a week to fix the damages."

The Mayor breathed a very deep sigh of disappointment and walked away.

The job took even longer than Mr. Captain expected. The damage was much greater than anyone initially realized. It was three full weeks before the boat was back in the water and ready to go. Those were twenty-one very long days for the Mayor. He lost all sense of excitement and achievement and joy. He still religiously spent time in the throne room, but every moment was consumed with pleading with the King to heal him of his burning, itching, growing red spots.

One morning, the Mayor woke up with terrible pain on the bottom of his feet. They were so sore that he was totally unable to walk.

"Oh no," he cried out in agony of soul and body. "Now I won't be able to accomplish anything for God! Now I won't be able to have any excitement in my life! What am I going to do?" The pain increased throughout the day. By the time the afternoon came around, the Mayor sent word for Dr. Whiz Dum to come right away. The doctor arrived late in the evening to find a miserable, suffering Mayor. After examining the patient, he carefully placed his tools back into his big, black bag, folded his hands together and stared at the pitiful looking Mayor.

After a few long minutes, the doctor finally spoke. "There's nothing else I can do," he flatly stated.

"But, can't you heal me?" the Mayor pleaded.

"Heal you!" the doctor blurted out in anger. "Heal you! Who do you think I am? Only God can heal! I only treat symptoms. You'd better just get used to your condition," he said coldly.

"You don't have to be so matter-of-fact about it," the Mayor blurted back.

"You're late at paying my last bill," the doctor said in anger, raising his voice more and more as he spoke. "I'm not going to treat you again until you pay the balance due. I'll be sending you this new bill tomorrow. I charge triple for house calls, and you'd better pay on time, or else!" He walked out of the room, slamming the door behind him.

This was the last thing the suffering Mayor needed. The physical agony, coupled with the lack of compassion shown him, caused the Mayor to cry out from the depths of his soul. Before he was finished, his good friend Mrs. Tender Mercy tapped on the door and entered the room. "Mayor Saved Soul," she began, "would you like for me to read some Psalms to you?"

The Mayor pulled himself up in the bed, and was about to tell her yes. He really wasn't up to a visit, but he didn't want to be rude to his faithful, compassionate friend.

"Oh, look," Mrs. Tender Mercy said as she lifted up the black bag belonging to Doctor Whiz Dum. "Your doctor must have left in a hurry. He forgot his bag," she said.

The name on the front of the bag caught the Mayor's attention. He noticed it said Dr. W. Whiz Dum. "I always thought Whiz was the Doctor's first name," he remarked. "But he's certainly not a whiz," he said as he stared at his horrible looking hands.

"My dear Mayor," Mrs. Tender Mercy tenderly began, "if only you had spoken to Mr. Comforter or the King about the doctor you've been seeing. They would have told you that his full name is Doctor Worldly Whiz Dum. What else would you expect from a doctor from the land of Mammon? You've looked to the world's methods for healing from your disease of discontentment, instead of looking to the Lord's ways."

"But I've accomplished great things for God," the Mayor argued. "I've found a lot of excitement and contentment in doing things for Him."

Mrs. Tender Mercy sat down on the edge of the Mayor's bed and continued. "The world says contentment is found in excitement and accomplishments. But, as you've painfully found out, it's only a temporary cure, at best."

She stood up and walked over to the window, looking out toward the stairway of faith which leads to the golden throne room. She then turned back towards the Mayor and spoke slowly and powerfully; indicating the words had first been engraved deep into her very soul. "True contentment is only found...in, with, and through the presence of King Jesus Christ." The words rang into the air like a crisp, clear sounding bell ringing out on a sunny, Sunday morning. Without saying another word she placed the black bag on the table near the window and left the room.

The Mayor turned over in the direction of that window, noticing the big black bag was completely blocking the nice view he usually had from there. The Mayor stared at the name on the bag for a long time. Doctor Worldly Whiz Dum! He wondered if Mrs. Tender Mercy purposely placed the bag there, or if it just happened that way. He knew that even if she didn't realize what she was doing, God allowed the black bag to block his view, just as surely as he had allowed the worldly doctor's advice to block him from true healing of the stubborn disease that was afflicting him.

"Lord Jesus, please help me. Even if I never get totally healed, I can't stand the thought of not being able to come into Your throne room again." He cried with deep tears for a long time. Finally, he expressed into the air the deep desire of his soul. "Oh, how I wish I could go into the throne room of my King!" he sighed. As soon as the words left his mouth Mr. Comforter entered the room and picked the Mayor up in his arms. Before he hardly knew what was happening, they were out of the house and on the road to the stairway of faith. As they entered the throne room, the angels were beginning a new worship song that they had just composed. Accompanying them were thousands upon thousands of harpists. The sound was absolutely beautiful. Mr. Comforter laid the Mayor down on the floor, right next to the throne.

Immediately, the Mayor began interrupting the service by screaming out to the Lord for healing. "Please, please, PLEASE HEAL ME!" he yelled. Mr. Comforter knelt down beside him and whispered into his ear, "Quit seeking your healing. Seek the Healer. Don't just seek the King's blessings. Seek Him. Seek His face, the face of your God."

"Oh. Okay," the humbled Mayor obediently replied. Ha-lle-luia, ha-lle-luia," the Mayor slowly began as he joined the flow of the heavenly worship. "Lord Jesus, I seek Your wonderful face, halleluia." Suddenly the cloud of selfishness around the Mayor dissolved away and he was then able to look up and clearly see the face of the King. Much to the Mayor's surprise, the King looked so very downcast, apparently in deep pain. As the Mayor laid there on the floor next to His feet he began a conversation with the Lord. "King Jesus, why are You so sad?"

"I'm in anguish over you, my dear Mayor Saved Soul," the King slowly answered.

"Over me!" he replied in shock.

"Yes," the King said, "and I have been for some time now. Ever since you began pulling up the weeds to build your all-consuming, front porch."

"But, why are you upset over me?" the dumbfounded Mayor asked.

"Well, for two reasons," the King said as He came down from the throne. He picked the sickly Mayor up in his arms and ascended with him back to His royal seat. "The first reason is...in all your afflictions, I too am afflicted." (Isaiah 63:9) He slowly caressed the Mayor's head with the love of a perfect parent. As all the Mayor's pain began to noticeably melt away, the King continued. "Secondly, I know that the contentment you have so diligently sought can only be found...in Me."

"But Lord," the relaxed Mayor replied, "I can't do anything for You, anymore. How could I possibly ever be content now?"

"By receiving My love, and returning that love back to Me," the King gently answered. "That's the reason why I created and redeemed you. That's your destiny, your highest calling: to know Me and My love for you, and to return that love back to Me."

"But Lord, the only way I know how to show You my love is by doing things for You and for others."

"Yes, I know that," the King lovingly acknowledged. "And I do remember and appreciate all the labor of love you have shown to Me through your many good deeds. But doing things for Me is only one way to express your love. It's not the greatest way, however. The greatest way is through worship."

"Through worship?" the Mayor asked. "Well, I can still do that!" he exclaimed, as hope began to rise up from within his tired heart. The Mayor then closed his eyes, leaned his head against the Lord's strong, supportive arms and tuned into the worship song the angels were singing to the King of kings. He became so caught up in worship that he got lost in God. He lost all track of time, and all awareness of his many problems. He even lost the awareness of himself as he was swallowed up in the realization and enjoyment of the majesty, glory and beauty of his King. For the first time in his life, his level of worship rose above the level of just singing songs. From the depths of his soul, he was expressing his love to his Lord as he relished in the sunshine of God's loving presence. It was a rich, intimate time of true heartfelt worship. Hours later, when the music died down, the Mayor was feeling strong enough to stand on his feet, with a little help from Mr. Comforter. The Mayor was undoubtedly getting better! He also knew that this would not just be a temporary cure.

Within a few weeks the Mayor was coming to the throne room three to four times a day; not to plead for anything, but just to worship the King. The worship got deeper and deeper, and more and more fulfilling. Even when he wasn't in the throne room he found himself singing songs to the Lamb as he began to live, on a regular basis, in His loving presence. The Mayor's heart was so focused on his Lord that he didn't even realize he was totally healed of the rash of discontentment until someone else first pointed it out to him.

CONCLUSION

One day, on the way to the throne room, Mr. Captain approached the Mayor and his faithful companion, Mr. Comforter.

"Mayor, am I glad to find you," Mr. Captain began. "I'm leaving Christian Island today. I wanted to say good-bye, and thanks for all you've done for me."

"Where are you moving to?" the Mayor asked with a little shock and a lot of disappointment.

"Well, I can't really say," the distressed captain said. "I'll send you a postcard once I'm settled." He suddenly turned and nearly ran away.

"Stop him," Mr. Comforter whispered into the Mayor's ear. "Something's not right and you need to find out what's happening with him."

The Mayor ran after his friend and caught up with him a few blocks away. "Mr. Captain, what's wrong?"

"Uh, nothing, sir," he abruptly answered without stopping. "I, I just have to leave."

The Mayor pursued him and lovingly grabbed his right hand. He noticed this caused intense pain to the nervous captain. The Mayor opened up Mr. Captain's hands and saw five or six red spots inside each hurting palm. "The rash of discontentment!" the Mayor announced.

"I'm sorry, sir," the captain said apologetically. "I've tried my best to be happy. I don't know why I'm not content. It just doesn't make sense. I have a wonderful wife and three lovely kids. I have a good job and I live on a great island. But for some reason the spots just keep getting more and more painful. I, I have to do something about it."

"So where are you going?" the Mayor lovingly demanded.

"I can't tell you. If I do, the doctor won't..." He stopped in mid-sentence, realizing he already said too much.

"Doctor Whiz Dum!" the Mayor remarked. "You're going to him, aren't you?"

The captain shook his head yes, and then decided to confess everything. "I went to him late last night when everyone was sleeping. He told me he used a very expensive medicine to cure you, and that it cost a thousand dollars per tablet. I told him I didn't have that kind of money, and I begged him to help me like he helped you. He offered to treat me for free, if I move to the coast of Mammon and become the captain of his private boat taxi service. But I don't know what to do now," he said as tears began to stream down his cheeks. "He told me that if I mentioned this to anyone, he would change his mind."

"Mr. Captain," the Mayor began. "Mr. Captain, listen to me. Have I ever lied to you?" The totally distraught captain shook his head no. "Mr. Captain, Doctor Worldly Whiz Dum did not cure me! King Jesus cured me! All the doctor could do was temporarily relieve my symptoms. He's lying to you. He's trying to make you his slave. He won't be able to heal you. I don't even think he's a real doctor. You'll be making a big mistake if you go to work for him."

"I don't want to work for him, sir," the captain replied. "I'm afraid I'd eventually become just like him; arrogant and hard. I wish I could be like you. I've seen such wonderful changes in your heart these past few months. Do you think the King that you serve could change my wicked heart?" he asked with tears beginning to flow down his face. The tears were over his sin-filled soul more than his pain-filled hands.

"Of course, Mr. Captain," the Mayor said as he gave him a reassuring hug. "Why don't you come with Mr. Comforter and I? We're going up to the throne room right now. We'll introduce you to King Jesus. He'll forgive you and heal you. You'll see. I promise, He will not disappoint you."

"Okay," the captain cautiously said. When they got to the first step of the stairway of faith the captain froze, not knowing if he could continue. Mr. Comforter put his arms around his shoulder, asking, "Mr. Captain, do you believe that King Jesus Christ is the Eternal Son of God?"

"Yes, I do," he confessed. "I believe He is. I truly believe, with all my heart!" The three of them continued, walking into the glorious throne room together. All the angels around the throne were noticeably jumping up and down in expressions of intense joy. Mr. Captain couldn't believe it when he was informed that they were all rejoicing over him! King Jesus came off his throne and walked over to them. Mr. Comforter stepped forward and said to the captain, "Mr. Captain, meet the Captain of captains, King Jesus. He is now the Captain of your salvation!"

The captain took one long look at the King and flew into His waiting arms. The King's embrace hugged the pain away and placed a new heart into the weary captain.

A few hours later Mayor Saved Soul, Mr. Captain and Mr. Comforter walked back to the steps leading down to Christian Island.

"I feel so good, so clean, so new!" Mr. Captain joyfully exclaimed. "There's only two things I'm concerned about, now" he added.

"What are they?" the happy Mayor asked as they all stopped about halfway down the stairs.

"I don't like my old name anymore," he replied. "Especially since it's already one of the King's names. He's the Captain of my salvation. I'm also not sure if my King would want me to take my next yearly trip around the world that's coming up soon.

Mr. Comforter then spoke up, saying, "Your new name shall be Mr. Witness, of Christian Island. The King told me to tell you that your first mission for Him is to witness throughout the world. Go ye therefore, into all the world and tell everyone who will listen that true contentment is only found in one place, in the presence of the King of Glory, the Lord Jesus Christ."

Mr. Witness opened his hands, noticing that all the painful red spots were completely gone! He lifted up his healed hands to the sky, yelling out extremely loud, "ALL GLORY, HONOR AND PRAISE TO THE KING OF KINGS, THE LORD OF LORDS, THE CAPTAIN OF MY SALVATION, THE ONLY TRUE SOURCE OF LASTING CONTENTMENT!" His voice echoed throughout the happy land of Christian Island.

"Hear the word of the Lord, O nations, and declare it to the isles afar off, and say, 'He who scattered Israel will gather him, and keep him as a shepherd does his flock.

For the Lord has redeemed Jacob, And ransomed him from the hand of one stronger than he. Therefore they shall come and sing in the height of Zion, streaming to the goodness of the Lord;

For wheat and new wine and oil, for the young of the flock and the herd; Their soul shall be like a well-watered garden, and they shall sorrow no more at all.

Then shall the virgin rejoice in the dance, and the young men and the old, together. For I will turn their mourning to joy, will comfort them, and make them rejoice rather than sorrow.

I will saturate the soul of the priests with

abundance, and My people shall be satisfied with My goodness, says the Lord." (Jeremiah 31:10-14 NKJV)

About The Author

Pastor Charles Simpson was raised in Tennessee and became a Christian in high school in the late 70's. Soon after graduating, he moved to New York City to be a missionary in the Big Apple. While on staff at Times Square Church he married his wife, Lynn. He has planted three churches: in the South Bronx, in Scottsdale, Arizona and in Astoria, Queens when he and his wife now live and pastor Hope Chapel, Queens Foursquare Church.

About Ordering This Book

Copies of this book can be conveniently purchased through the Internet site of Amazon books which is www.amazon.com. Type in the book name and follow the directions.

Or this book can be purchased through Ascribe Publishing. The price is $10.00 per book, which will pay all costs, including taxes, shipping and handling. A check or money order should be made out to Ascribe Publishing, P.O. Box 5726, L.I.C., NY, 11105. Call (718) 932-3732 for quantity discounts or visit our web site at:
http://homestead.juno.com/ascribepublishing
(Bookstores can order from Spring Arbor
Distributors at 1-800-395-5599.)

Also Available From Ascribe Publishing:

Angel Lucifer – Evil's Origin

"Since He is all-powerful, then why does God allow so much suffering and heartache to take place in this world in which we live?"

"If God is the Creator of all, does this mean He is the Author of evil?"

These questions and more are addressed in this action-packed novel about an anointed angel who turns into the enemy of God. Using the Biblical glimpses of his downfall as our framework, I paint a picture of Lucifer's amazing, catastrophic transformation.

(ISBN 0-97000-48-0-X, 187 pgs., $9.99)